T0199225

# THE SPY
# WHO COULDN'T SAY NO

A Cocktail of Romance, Intrigue and Murder

L. A. WIGGINS

authorHOUSE®

*AuthorHouse™*
*1663 Liberty Drive*
*Bloomington, IN 47403*
*www.authorhouse.com*
*Phone: 1 (800) 839-8640*

*Published by AuthorHouse 08/13/2015*

*ISBN: 978-1-5049-2778-9 (sc)*
*ISBN: 978-1-5049-2779-6 (e)*

*Library of Congress Control Number: 2015912640*

*Print information available on the last page.*

# Contents

# Prologue

Billy Wright's paid agents, who became close associates, were still in place in and around Prague, Leipzig and London. And they were keeping an eye on adversarial suspects. The ASA and CIA, with their need for Wright's covert services of extracting assets, secret documents or targets from the other side of the Iron Curtain, made allowances for his unorthodox ways. They gave him a free hand to carry out his assignments. His superiors did try to curtail his somewhat aggressive reactions to dangerous situations, which did save his life several times.

Keeping an eye on possible embryonic sleeper cells in Cambridge was as important as the extractions of high value targets. From a rented flat being used as his ops center, his work was as risky as any covert assignments. KGB agents were trying to hunt him down and extract him and his past targets back to Leipzig or Russia. These were the children of defecting assets, who were used in luring their scientist parents to the West. These sons and daughters were also to be used by the Soviets to lure back the defectors to finish their work in the jet propulsion base where they were confined.

Sandwiched between foreign assignments, his focus was on the CIA's main goal of obtaining the names of easily manipulated future British civil servants who were attending Cambridge and Oxford, or what is known as the Ox-Bridge connection. Billy had put together a few of his own likeminded students to infiltrate the infamous Apostle Society, along with a network of his handpicked operators in two Soviet Bloc countries.

Two of Billy's associates in the United Kingdom are young defectors from behind the Curtain, to a trusted London Cockney taxi driver, and past and present CIA field covert agents. Wright's uncanny ability of reading people is a true gift, or as General Thibodeau once commented, "Young Wright has a God-given knack of foretelling danger."

Billy's ops centers in Cambridge, Leipzig and Prague are operational and efficient. His skills of avoiding being grabbed partly come from his grappling with older brothers in back yard wrestling matches during his youth. He would study their moves, and pre-empt any attempt to subdue him. The Soviet authorities or secret police had no real idea of Billy's identity as they tried many times to obtain his photograph. However, they do keep track of his infiltration points into porous border areas where he would enter using the Czechoslovakian forest as cover. In the past year there had been six Czech soldiers and two Russian officers killed in and around the border by a suspected American agent.

Back in Cambridge a dossier was being kept by the local police, and it was shared with Britain's MI5 and MI6; it had to do with the murder of a suspected KGB agent. An American agent was suspected of working covertly (with no authorization) the Cambridge area. Maybe it had to do with the security of the two large American air bases that were close-by. This information was leaked to General Thibodeau in the American Embassy as to why Whitehall would suspect the CIA of being involved, and it was unnerving. Billy would be called by Thibodeau to set up briefings away from London or Cambridge.

When a sensitive covert assignment was finalized, the meetings would be held on a remote island on Florida's West Coast. This is where Billy Wright would have the chance to either agree or amend the strategy. It was important that these plans had no chance of being compromised by someone spying on them or from dispatches leaked through the London Embassy.

Leos Novak was used to persuade his parents to defect a few months later. Herr Novak and his wife were working in a guarded rocket propulsion laboratory in Leipzig as scientists for the Soviet space program, when Wright escorted them out of the East. The Americans wanted their services as much as the Russians.

Another part of this puzzle was Monika and her parents, who had grown up with the Novak's in the same compound. After freeing the three associates of the Novak's by Wright bringing them through the deep Bohemian Forest bordering West Germany, Monika was granted a place at Cambridge University. Leos and Monika were now working for Wright and the CIA in monitoring all anti-American activities in Great Britain.

Wright's boyish looks were ideal in sending him into communist enclaves, masquerading as a student. Billy was an astute and stealthy hunter in his childhood, which has afforded him a sixth sense of impending danger to a point of having a gift of clairvoyant qualities.

With an happenstance of finding Gypsies in a flea market in Prague to work with, from money laundering to having someone who knew the back roads around Prague and past road blocks was an unbelievable piece of luck. As the Gypsies were adversaries of the dreaded secret police, it was a stroke of genius for Wright to gain their trust and become ensconced inside Gypsy villages in Berlin, Prague and Leipzig.

# Chapter 1

## Risky Assignment

Wright was summoned to the London Embassy for a briefing with the CIA Director from Washington, retired General Thibodeau, the now London Director General Jerald (Jerry) Simpson and the ASA Director General Frank Neuhofer from Frankfurt. The three present or past generals used a three-way conference call to go over a predetermined plan for the benefit of Captain Wright. Wright was told his next assignment was to once again extract two scientists from under the same Stasi guarded complex in Leipzig. These targets were to be delivered somewhere in the West within the next few weeks or as soon as possible depending on circumstances.

The general's mentioned during this briefing that there was one small problem. The two assets had a daughter who had to accompany them on their defection. The three would have to be kept in a group, so to convey to each other that they were all going to be taken to the West together. The parents would not go without the daughter or the daughter her parents.

General Thibodeau asked over the speaker, "Wright, you have been expecting this assignment for several months to be put into motion. Do you have a plan ready to go if we decide to carry on?"

"Yes sir, I have thought about a plan many times; however, one problem crops up in every scenario. That problem is, excuse me for using a metaphor, but I may have gone to the same well too many times for this to work successfully. My contact with the secret police in Prague concurs that this would be a very dangerous assignment since the Stasi in Leipzig would certainly be on the lookout for me next time."

General Neuhofer from Frankfurt added his concerns, "Captain, Is there any way we could help you to make sure you will succeed, other than having the Bad Aibling team at the border?"

"Yes there is general, I will need two Russian passports with the names of Colonel Augustus Wolf. That's Wolf without an 'e' and Vlad Volgof for the first sergeant, if he is allowed to help me. The second and most important thing that will be needed is night vision or infrared goggles, similar to the ones we had in basic training. The last item is $10,000 Yankee dollars in $100 note bills. I normally like to work alone, but this time I may need someone who speaks fluent Russian to go with me. The Stasi will not be looking for two of us as my MO depicts a lone wolf, pardon the pun."

General Simpson spoke about his concerns and misgivings. "Wright, the first sergeant, being a married man, adds a little more gravity to the situation. You will be in command and he will be in your care."

"Generals, you won't have to worry about the first sergeant even though it does add pressure to the situation; he is a seasoned soldier as you all know. However, we may have to wait a few extra days if you are not able to deliver all the tools needed in a timely manner."

Thibodeau said, "OK Wright, go back to Cambridge University and we will let you know when and where you need to be. Also, a backup plan is already in motion for you to go to the University of Berlin as an exchange student or wherever the daughter of the assets is going to school. We will have two passports made up for you, and one for the first sergeant if he is available. I want you in Brighton at the usual place this weekend, and bring your girlfriend so she can visit with Mrs. T. You can go now and we will be in contact as soon as the plans are finalized from Washington."

Before heading back to university, it was possible to make my way towards the underground and surprise my fiancé Nicola as she gets out of school, where she teaches in Harrow on the Hill.

No sooner did I walk out of the embassy doors when a large black London taxi drove up and the driver said, "Where you edded, Guv?"

It was Kenny, my old Cockney helper. I was about to say where I was going when he interrupted me before uttering the first word.

"Ya goin to see that girl of yours wot lives in 'arrow on the 'ill, ain't ya Guv. Get in, I'll take you since it's raining."

"Thanks Kenny. Yes, I will hopefully spend the night in Harrow and take her out for a show and dinner. Is there anything happening around the old manor?"

"Since you mentioned it, Guv, the Russian geezer 'as been seen with the 'igh ups in your embassy. I reckon there is something not right about the goings on wif those two who supposed to be unfriendly at the best of times."

"Thank you for that bit of news Kenny, keep it under your hat for a few months and I will act on it when the time is right."

"Will do, Guv. Working on something at the moment that needs your attention, do ya Guv. Now wot about that pretty young lady of yours, I thought you two were getting itched soon."

I was about to say something when Kenny shouted at Nicola coming through the school gate, "Needing a lift luv?"

When Nicola saw me in the back of Kenny's cab she smiled, folded her umbrella, and scooted close to give me a kiss after Kenny opened the back door for her to climb in.

She said, "Thank you Kenny, what a lovely surprise, the children will be impressed, not to mention the others teachers. Now Billy, what are you doing in Harrow, hope you're not playing hooky from university."

I was about to answer in when Kenny chimed in, "I caught 'im coming out of the compound 'avin' a meetin' wif the general luv."

"What did the general want to see you about Billy?"

Kenny was looking at me in his rear view mirror, watching me squirm. I'm trying to say something just as we get to 24 Harley Crescent, Nicola's house, in the nick of time. Kenny drove away laughing, probably at how I looked while trying to explain to Nicola what was said at the briefing a few hours ago.

Nicola's father opens the door saying, "Well blow me; is that Kenny?" We both told him it was and while I was in London using his services, he gave me a lift out here.

She told her dad, "Billy had an appointment at the embassy and decided to visit us, hopefully staying for the night. Billy was about to tell me why he was called to the embassy when we arrived."

Nicola and her dad were waiting for me to say something. He got tired of waiting so he put the kettle on for a cup of tea. Nicola and I were in the lounge when her dad called out to say the tea was ready.

As we sat on the couch Jack said, "Well then, when and where are you off to next me ol son."

I quietly said, *"Eastern Europe."*

Hoping that would be enough information to have them drop the subject.

Her father said as he sipped his tea and dunked a shortbread biscuit, "I told you before Nic, he's a bleeding spy, didn't I me ol kid."

"Sir, I don't like telling untruths or being put in a position where I have to stretch the truth. I know you all need more information about me since I want to marry your daughter."

"By the way son, a letter came for you today, I think it's for you. It is addressed to a Captain Wright, all the way from Washington."

Nicola was speechless to think I was still in the Army and a captain at that. Oh brother, this was not going to be easy to explain away.

"Billy, I thought when you were commissioned to be a first lieutenant, and was only an honorable posting, not a formal rank," she said.

"Look Nicola, I am unofficially out of the Army; however, every man in the States has to serve a six-year term. The last three years of this obligation are for the ones who volunteered, and were not drafted; it is known as inactive duty. The general and his wife want me in Brighton this weekend and asked if you were free to go also."

"Sure Billy, I think that would be exciting. Why is the General coming over to see you?"

"I guess to talk over some type of logistics."

Nicola and her dad were completely confused by my answer, and went on to get the evening meal ready for Flo who was at work. Both of them had decided they have heard enough of my explanation, and asked me to do something useful such as setting the table.

The next day I had to leave by 5 a.m. to catch a train that would get me to Cambridge in time for the first class. There was just enough time to go to the apartment and get changed. Two notes were on the kitchen table asking for me to meet Leos, and another one to meet David at the university cafeteria this morning. I had to hurry to see what David wanted. Leos was probably the most crucial to see, and we were to meet at the train station cafe around 4 p.m.

David was about to give up on me as he seemed to need to leave when I walked into the dining hall. He had me a cup of tea ready, which was probably cold by now.

He frantically asked, "Where have you been Billy, we need your advice on what to do about a new professor who is taking over the Apostle's society agenda."

"Alright David, let's get together with Leos at 7 p.m., and talk about our strategy over a pint."

That was taken care of for the moment, no doubt Leos was most likely wanting to discuss the same problem. David was a fellow I worked with last summer while punting the tourists up and down the river Cam. We both worked for a colorful gentleman, who is a CIA operative masquerading as the boat rentals owner. Burt had been an associate of General Thibodeau's in the past while working in the field as a British and American spy.

Meeting Leos at 4 p.m. was fortuitous. He had information on the new university Don, and his plans to go to an East German University with several students immediately at the start of their fall semester. He wants as many of the Apostle members to go, as well as three lovely girls. After thanking him for the information, we agreed to meet David at 7 p.m.

That evening I got to the cafe a few minutes early to buy the drinks and find a suitable table to have this meeting. Leos and David walked in together, and started telling me they were asked to go to Berlin with the professor in two weeks. Both of them did not want to go as they had things to do with their girlfriends before the Christmas holidays, and Leos wanted to go to the States to be with his parents as did his girlfriend Monika.

"Go ahead and sign up for the three-month exchange trip. You will not have to go as I will work out your excuses later this week. This may work out for all of us with me being a replacement."

"I have a meeting this weekend that will probably have me ordered on to a new assignment, and taking me out of here for up to three months. This student exchange business may be a good thing for me to use as a cover. I will let you both know on Monday. Leos, if you went to Berlin, you would not come back, and the professor most likely knows that, my feeling is he will try to help the KGB with getting you back to the East."

# Chapter 2

## The CIA Memorandum

Nicola and I arrived in Brighton on Friday night after leaving Harrow as soon as school let out. Kenny drove us in his taxi to pick up his wife as it was on the way, and we were all guests of the CIA and General Thibodeau for the weekend.

The general was notified that we were all signing in and came down to say that dinner was being served in 30 minutes in the grand dining room.

After getting all dolled up, we all went down together. Mrs. Thibodeau arranged the seating with me between her and the general, and Nicola on his other side.

The general leaned over and said, "Wright, we will talk tomorrow. I want to see you at 0700 down here. Mother will be in charge of getting us all together for breakfast around 9."

"Yes sir."

Nicola leaned around the general and smiled as she mimed, "see you later darling." The evening was a lot of fun with great food and Kenny telling us about the different characters he had ferried around his turf. Music started up with Nicola urging me to dance as we were in the lounge by now.

I said, "Nicola, with no one else dancing, everyone will see how lousy I am at dancing."

"Oh darling, you will do just fine, I want to dance with you."

I got up to go get more drinks to get out of dancing as Kenny said, "You go on the dance floor Guv, I'll get wot everyone wants."

"Thanks Kenny, for helping out again."

The general barked out, "Kenny, put the drinks on my room."

Needless to say Nicola and I danced all night, leaving the old folks to entertain each other.

The next morning, I was hoping to be down in the dining room early so the general wasn't kept waiting. He was already at a table far away in the corner giving a waiter his order. I heard him say to just bring double the order; he will have the same as me.

Thibodeau did not waste any time, saying, "This official briefing is courtesy of the agency as they are paying the bill. I thought that Kenny should also be rewarded for all the help he gives you. He doesn't seem to be working for me or General Simpson as he is loyal to only you Wright, even though we pay his wages."

The CIA Director was being officious and said "You will be going on an assignment that is going to require a lot of luck and meticulous planning by yourself, if you want to stay alive. You were told what to expect quite awhile ago and I hope you have started thinking about a plan.

"We have the names of the three assets who will need your help in coming over to our side. If you are caught we will say you went rogue and were free lancing. There will be no attempt to buy you out or barter for your release in any type of situation. If you are successful in escaping, you had better do it quickly or we will think you have been turned by the Stasi"

"The longer you are held captive, if you do get caught, you will be tortured, drugged and your close friends or relatives will be threatened. The Soviets will use any tool to get you to talk, and I promise after a period of time you will talk. The longer you are silent from us, we will deem you are dead. If you miraculously show up months later we will assume you have crossed over. Do you have any questions on the assignment?"

"Yes sir. You didn't ask if I had decided to take the job on."

"Don't start playing games with me Wright. You know there is no one else who can do this job. What do you want if you are still alive in three months?"

"Well sir, I would like to be promoted to captain and have another month on the beach in Florida. I heard about a desolate island called Little Gasparilla where the beaches are pristine."

"That is no problem. Now how much money do you need to carry out the mission with a little excursion to spy on a Russian city in the Czech Republic?"

"Like I said before, $10,000 in $100 notes."

"The money will be ready by the time you arrive in West Germany. Now, if there is any money leftover you will have to turn it back in when you get back."

"General, I will be frugal and hope to have some of the funds to turn in as soon as I return."

"Yeah right, I was told you may impersonate a Russian Colonel in your plans. You will be shot if you caught wearing another uniform."

"General, I would be shot if I dressed as a ballerina."

Thibodeau burst out laughing just as everyone else appeared.

Mrs. T asked, "Tibby, are you boys telling naughty jokes. You must keep those things away from us ladies." She was very Southern in the way she talked.

The general was laughing so much he had a hard time answering her. His actions made all of us join in laughing, even though it was not appreciated by others having breakfast in the same dining room.

Finally the general said, "Mother, with what Wright told me, I could not conjure up the image he portrayed without laughing."

Thibodeau quickly excused himself as he headed for the washroom, laughing as he went.

I stood up and apologized to everyone in the room, "My friend is a general and he and I are so sorry our raucousness flooded into your areas."

The general returned and told everyone that Wright once was dressed as a ballerina at some costume party. He then started laughing again as tears streamed down his face.

Mrs. Thibodeau said, "Tibby, remember your heart condition, you mustn't overdo anything."

Most of the patrons eating were weekenders, and after hearing why the general was so loud with his explanation started in on the laughter. They couldn't know if he was talking about Kenny or me. It was nice seeing everyone now enjoying the situation and trying to figure out who Wright was.

Later that day with naps out of the way and the three ladies shopping in the lanes, the general found me sitting on a bench on the pier. Even though the sun was out, the breeze blowing off the sea was cold enough for us to have out trench coats wrapped around us. I had a minute to think what is it he would want to talk about.

Thibodeau said, "Wright, there is something we need to discuss before I head back to Washington.

This is unfortunate that you have the responsibility to get this job done before returning home, even if Christmas has to be delayed on your part."

"What could be as important as me being with Nicola on Christmas morning, sir?"

"... You have a mission as or more important than extracting the three assets from behind the Iron Curtain. The Russians are building a new city and secret military base 30 miles northeast of Prague next to a village called Milovice. The rumor is that this facility will be used for storing nuclear weapons. We need to know it's true location, its name and how many barracks are being built."

"Now general, how am I going to handle two missions in the same period of time without being discovered?"

"If you are successful in getting the three assets across and you have scouted out this new Russian city before Christmas, I will arrange for you and Nicola to go to Florida during her Christmas break and then again during the Easter break. The 30 days you wanted to be on that island will be awarded along with a promotion. When you are in Florida, the wife and I will have to spend the odd weekend with you. This will ensure the agency has a reason for paying your expenses as you will brief me on your assignments, and then we will talk about your next mission in the April briefing that I will give you."

"Alright sir, that's a deal if it is first class on both trips."

"Harrumph, you are impertinent Wright. I will see what I can do."

"Thank you sir.'

Now Kenny is walking over. Ask him who he is working for, you or me."

Kenny said, "Guv, general, mind if I join you? Nice day innit."

The general responded. "Yes it is Kenny, a braw day it is. Now look Kenny, please do not be offended, I need to know why you never give me any information like you freely give to Wright."

"Well sir, if you don't mind me saying like, I don't trust you Yanks that much."

Thibodeau said, "What impertinence, I am leaving; you two can have the bench."

When Thibodeau was out of sight, and we could talk freely for the first time in two days, Kenny asked.

"How did I do Guv?"

"On script Kenny, well done."

"Will he be sore Guv?"

"For a short time, but he will remember not to press you for information that may get you in trouble with Simpson, the ambassador and the KGB agent. What is the old English saying when trouble arrives, being 'in a pickle.'?"

"That's the one Guv. Am I right or am I reading you wrongly, that the general is not to know wot I'm seeing with me own eyes."

"For now or if I don't come back from the next mission, then you will have to divulge everything you know from day one, and what we had discussed over the last year."

Kenny was taken aback that there was actually danger in my assignments, which may hamper a return to London. The general left a note for me to meet him in the morning at 0600 for breakfast before he took off for Heathrow. With this information, I ran down Kenny and asked him to drive the general and his wife to the airport after breakfast. Nicola and I would rather catch the train back to Harrow so we could be alone.

The next morning the meeting with Thibodeau went as planned. When we sat down and after the waiter left I said, "General Thibodeau, I am responsible for the way Kenny spoke to you like he did. I told him to do exactly as he did. He was reluctant at first and did not want to be disrespectful to you. After I explained the reasons for me asking him to carry out my orders was to protect you and General Simpson. I thought it was best that certain observations not be included in CIA dispatches through the embassy mail system or by phone. Nor did I think it was wise to have these clandestine operations concerning the ambassador and the KGB agent, put into a report that would go through the ambassador's office."

"Wright, do I hear you right? You have the taxi driver in your confidence and you keep three generals in the dark on your covertness in London."

"No general, Kenny has no idea what I was thinking or why it was imperative you be kept out of the mix. This is a concern of mine that I suspect the ambassador to be in bed with the Russians, just a hunch that goes with his associations with different KGB agents during the last year. These allegations cannot be substantiated until more work is done on this problem or until I return from the next two missions to present the evidence. Kenny will hand over all of our correspondence and summations if I do not return by early next year."

"Wright, you think the phone lines are not secure in the embassy. Who would have a tap on them?"

"Let's see general if it behooves the ambassador to have them tapped if he is being naughty and covering his tracks. What if the British know he is bent; they will want to know how much is being talked about concerning their own security. In the past year the ambassador had left the building several times to use a phone box a mile away, and then walk back to the embassy; need I say more?"

"I see Wright. You seem to have a knack to state the obvious or you are just lucky in putting a sentence together that makes sense. The ladies and the driver are coming. I am comfortable now in your actions and we can talk when you get back in about three months."

L. A. Wiggins

The briefing was over and we all enjoyed breakfast with a lot of good feelings. The six of us always have enjoyed the comradeship that seemed to be prevalent when we all got together. Kenny, his wife, and the Thibodeau's left Nicola and I at the table as they left for the airport.

We stayed for another cup of tea and some quite honest talk about our future as husband and wife. I managed to put my apprehension about our future as a married couple at least for the next 12 months in a way that Nicola understood was, for her own good. She was worried that my luck would run out one day and she would never see me again. I told her more than I should have about the nasty people in other countries, who wouldn't tolerate someone like me crossing into their area.

The train ride to London gave us time to work out a Christmas schedule. This is the last chance we would talk for a while. It really was too hard to tell her how I looked forward to new assignments.

The next morning walking Nicola to her school was full of quiet regret for both of us. We didn't seem to mind the drizzle as we hated to say good-bye to each other.

When I arrived back in the Cambridge, there was a note on the dining table from Leos. He needed to see me asap in the university cafeteria that morning. Leos was sitting by himself with a pot of tea ready for us to have with a stack of biscuits. He got up and started walking towards me when he saw the new professor and his wife jostle me as they brushed past on both sides. He was evidently in a hurry to speak to him. The professor didn't turn around to see who he almost bowled over.

The next table to them was empty, so I grabbed a cup of tea from the counter and positioned myself with my back to them so I could hear what they were saying. This professor or Don was the one who was now over- seeing the Apostles. He was very upset that I was an alternate on the foreign student exchange list going to Berlin University. The man was adamant that no one on the list "no showed" and then have Ludwig take their place. He went on to excoriate me in a way that would make a priest blush. He handed Leos his airline ticket and left to get to his first lecture, leaving his wife to give him traveling instructions and pocket money in East German Marks.

The Don's wife started teasing Leos by asking if he had a girlfriend and if she was going on the trip. She made it quite clear that she was going to be available while they all were in Berlin. She also mentioned that her husband had set up meetings with the local authorities, and would spend time with several Russian Party Members during the three months.

Needless to say, we didn't have time to talk and managed to mime that we could meet at the train station at our usual time of 4 p.m. She was still hitting on Leos when I left the room. My class with the new Don, Rodney, was most interesting, especially when I raised my hand to say something when he was talking about the Berlin trip. He ignored my gesture and kept on as the rest of the class thought he was rude. I wanted to provoke him in front of everyone, but he didn't take the bait.

That afternoon I waited for Leos with two cups of coffee in the station cafe as he was unusually late by almost half an hour. He looked okay when he sat down and started drinking the cold coffee.

Leos started with, "Can you believe the professor's wife. Soon after you left she started rubbing my leg with her leg and wanted to hold hands."

"Forget about her Leos, she will go away; now, what was it you wanted to see me about this morning?"

"Monika was asked to also be a stand-in if someone drops out. She is considering going if there is room for her."

"I will talk to her about it when I get back to the flat. Tell Monika not to fix supper tonight as I will stop and get some fish and chips. I have to go to see David at the pub."

"One other item Billy, the KGB agent will be here this Friday for a meeting."

It was suspect that the Russian from London wanted a meeting before the members took off for East Germany. David was early and waiting with a couple pints of beer at the bar. He was glad to see me walk in as if I wasn't going to be around one of these days.

David said, "I guess you heard that the new Don doesn't want you on the trip as he is making sure no one drops out and thus letting you in."

"Yeah, I know. We have a bigger problem in that Monika wants to go with your group, and I know she wouldn't be coming back if she went."

"What are you going to do Billy? She will not be swayed if I am reading her intentions correctly."

"I really don't know now since you have told me that bit of news. I will have to think of something in the next 30 minutes. Come back with me and have some supper, we can both try to dissuade her."

"Sorry mate, I have a date, you have to do it all by yourself; let me know how you do tomorrow."

It was important to stop at a phone box to call General Thibodeau in Washington about Monika, and the problem of her wanting to go on the exchange. Luck was with me as he answered his phone, and when after explaining to him that Monika was asked to go to East Berlin with some of her classmates his phone went dead. I thought to myself this was no time to be cut off.

After waiting a minute, hoping we would be reconnected, he then asked, "Since you will be taking the place of Leos, would she like to come see her parents and have Leos come, too? I will get the airplane tickets as soon as you let me know.

When is the next school recess? No, wait; let's have them here for Christmas and leave Cambridge by December 12."

"Good thinking, sir; I will tell them tonight and let you know if they would like to do that. You do seem to know how to get me out of a pickle. I have to go sir; the beeps are going off in the phone box."

With that the phone went dead, this time for good.

I bought a bottle of Liebfraumilch to celebrate them going to see their parents. The two defectors were waiting as they held hands and were caught cuddling in the kitchen. They were embarrassed when I walked in with a purposeful cough. Monika laid the table as Leos opened the wine and poured it into three tumblers up to the brim.

It didn't take long for us to get to the subject of the trip. Monika was adamant about going since Rodney, the professor, had personally asked her to join his group. Her fears were that her grades may be affected by telling him she did not want to go. He may see the refusal as her being disrespectful of his authoritarian position.

When Monika took a breath and started to say something else, it gave me the chance to pitch my best rebuttal on why she should stay home. I advised her to tell Professor Rodney Chesterton North that she would like to go since Leos her friend was going to be in the same group. Leos looked a little upset at me saying it would be alright for her to go. Now I have to be careful not to put a damper on both of their wishes and concerns by telling them why I felt this was a good idea. They were both looking at me silently as they both were enjoying the fish and chips. The ploy was to have them have as much wine as possible before getting into the reasons.

With the food gone and the wine almost finished I said, "Monika, Leos, your early grades will be assessed before the group takes off. If you both no-show it will be too late for your marks to be affected. Now saying that Monika, I have concerns about you going to a Soviet Bloc country so soon after your parents had defected to America. Let's just say you both are going for the time being or until it can be proven that the trip is not a good idea. If you agree to wait until this weekend to make your decision, it would be appreciated by me."

Leos said, "Waiting until the weekend to let the professor know is being a bit underhanded. The professor and his wife are having a party for the students who are booked to go. Some tickets and instructions will be handed out on Friday night during the get together at the same pub that David works at. We would probably feel like we were being deceitful and may show our feelings through our actions or expressions, if we knew we were in on the deception. We will do as you like since you always seem to have our best interest in mind."

With the discussion now put off until the weekend, we cleaned up the dishes and headed for our bedrooms. The next morning in North's class, he made the announcement about the party and at the same time asked me to see him in his office after the bell rings.

In his office as he peered over his glasses, he said in a sarcastic way, "So sorry Ludwig to inform you that everyone on the list has confirmed that they will be traveling with the group to Berlin, so you will not need to attend our party."

Not letting him bait me into a confrontation by being overly nice to him was worth the look on his slender face.

After telling him I understood he said, "Before you leave, do you know any Yanks attending Cambridge or Oxford called Billy?"

"No sir, the only Yank I ever heard of by that name was Billy the Kid. I think he is dead, sir."

As I walked through the door I turned around to see he had a contented smirk on his face.

David was waiting for me at the corner of the building before heading off to another class. We agreed to meet back at my flat at lunch as he had something to tell me that couldn't wait any longer.

David was at the flat before I got there, and munching on some leftover chips from the night before. He was feeling bad since his girlfriend was furious he was going on the trip.

He said, "There is an emergency meeting Friday before the party at the professor's house for the members of the Apostle Club. The Russian agent will be in town for that meeting, but will not stay for the party. This is going off the reason for me wanting to see you; we were all invited for an impromptu Thursday night cocktail party to discuss why the Russian wanted to see everyone going on the trip. Now, will you be in Berlin when the group arrives?"

"Yes, I will be at the reception in Berlin. If you get a chance Thursday night at the professor's house, go to the bathroom on the ground floor and unlatch the window. It would be better to unlock the lounge doors leading into the garden if you get the chance. Now don't go into the garden as this will ensure the doors will be checked when you all leave for the party. Why do you need to know about my being in Berlin?"

"Billy, I would like to earn the money that the agency is paying me as it seems that I am not doing enough to compensate you and the general. Can you use me in any way to help in your work in Germany?

I will let you know. Let's get back for the afternoon class before we are late."

Friday was here in a hurry with only a few days left before I had to be in Bad Aibling Saturday afternoon. There was a lot to do today with school in the morning, and then meeting Kenny at Kings Cross Station at 2 p.m. I then had to get back to Cambridge to see Leos and Monika.

Kenny was jawing with another taxi driver as he waited for me.

After getting into his cab he asked, "Where to Guv, to see the general?"

"No Kenny, to the Russian's flat."

"Right Guv, it so happens you just missed him. He is on is way to sheep land. I would guess Guv, you want to rearrange is papers."

"Yes I do Kenny. I hope the key still works."

"No such luck Guv, the locks were changed from the last time you helped him according to me friend that cleans the place, 'owever I noticed 'e did leave a key under the mat for a lady of the night, if you catch my drift."

I wasn't sure what I was looking for and hoped to stumble onto something useful. Kenny was to wait and blow the horn if anyone suspicious went to the door. I was in looking around when I noticed the spare bedroom door ajar. Looking inside, I saw a young lady in bed. After studying her for a short time I realized it was a young Scottish girl that looked familiar. It was Arabella, who had worked in Cambridge before the police ran her away.

Sounds were coming from the room Arabella was in, and spotting some papers on the desk and a locked briefcase under the desk made me hurry to want to get out quickly. After grabbing the briefcase and rolling up the papers into a tidy roll, I left. I left the front door open on purpose, hoping she would call the police so they would mess things up and the KGB agent wouldn't know who to blame.

Back in the taxi Kenny said, "Didn't take you long Guv."

"There was a young lady sleeping off working the late shift, if you know what I mean, Kenny."

"Right, I know the one, she kips out there on occasions."

I couldn't wait to get back to my flat to see what was in the case and what kind of papers I'd collected. Kenny drove me back to Cambridge and we said our goodbyes until the next time. He was going to keep an eye out for the Russian and the ambassador for me.

Back at the flat with no one around I went through the briefcase after prying open the lock with a screwdriver to discover an envelope with over 5,000 in 20 pound notes. Notes in Russian were hard to decipher except for the names of William Wright, the ambassador, Leos Novak and Monika Kroupa. Maybe Leos knows enough Russian to see what these papers were all about.

It was time to go to the professor's house to snoop around. Around the back, the door off the garden was locked, but the bathroom window was unlocked. Moving a wooden bench was essential to get me where I could bend over the opened window on my stomach. The professor's office was in an extra bedroom or box room upstairs. The curtains were drawn so it was not risky to turn on the lights. I sat at his desk and in the long drawer was a dossier on each student. The files on me, Leos and Monika were taken, along with two passports belonging to him and his wife. In a side locked drawer, which was easy to open with his envelope opener, was a large file full of Russian correspondence.

My heart was beating wildly, which usually meant it was time for me to get out. Just as I climbed out the window the front door opened with car's headlights cascading towards the back of the house. Closing the window gently, I stepped onto the ground and placed a piece of paper from the Russian's briefcase behind the bench for the police to find.

Leos and Monika were in my flat when I got there.

I said, "Glad you are here, how did the party go?"

They both said at the same time, "It was okay, not much fun listening to the professor going over our agenda for the three months in East Berlin. The Russian was creepy as he kept staring at the two of us. He had to leave almost as fast as he got there with some type of emergency."

I handed Leos and Monika the dossier on us from the Russian's briefcase. He looked perplexed as to where did I get these items.

"Alright Leos, read these documents that are in Russian and let me know what they say."

By the way, Leos changed expressions as he perused the file gave Monika and me a feeling that there was something wrong, especially when he nervously asked one of us to make him a cup of tea. More and more perspiration was collecting on his forehead the longer he read the documents.

Leos put down the files and told Monika, "We are not to go to Berlin for any reason. These documents describe where and when we both were to be apprehended by the KGB. It was to be at a reception given for the English students the first evening there. Our Professor Rodney is working with the London KGB agent. Billy, the only reason you have not been killed is because they have no idea who you are or what you look like. They think you are attending Oxford under an assumed name, possibly a Czech or German alias."

Monika was shaken to know that she would have been taken as a prisoner and her parents would have to return to Leipzig.

I spoke up and said to the both, "The general wanted your decision on you flying to America to spend Christmas with your parents. What can I tell him?"

They got up, hugged me, and told me to tell him, "Yes, please."

"Okay team, we have to bundle these documents up and I will mail them out in the morning at the airport. Now when David and I are gone, you are in charge by keeping the surveillance going around the campus. We may be back in a month to three months, according to how things work out over there.

"Now listen, this is most important. On the evening before you are due to leave on the school trip, you will come down with a flu virus as to not show suspicion that you know something is up. Monika, when the professor or his wife come over to see if you really are sick, get out of bed and pretend to get dressed. As you get dressed fall over simulating a weak and frail body. Do not bath or wash for two days and put a little oil on your face and have the heat turned up as high as the furnace will allow you have it. I guarantee you he or she will be out of here in a flash and telling you to stay home. Is that clear?"

They both said that they would practice being sick so it will look genuine.

Leos asked, "Billy, what do we do if you are killed or captured?"

Monika said, "Leos, how could you think of such a horrible thing like that?"

"He is right Monika; I should have some type of instructions for you to follow. I will write the phone number of someone to call, only if you cannot get a hold of the general in the London Embassy. The phone number will be behind the bathroom mirror, but not on the wall where it could be found. I have to call the general now from my room and then get to sleep. I will be out before you wake up and will see you in less than three months or when you get back from the States. Now, good night."

After a goodbye kiss from Monika, I went to my room to pack and call the general with the good news. While packing I hid the Russian's gun in among my tee shirts and underwear.

# Chapter 3

## Billy Becomes Will

I arrived in Frankfurt the next morning and picked up my car at the ASA headquarters. Even though it was a Saturday, General Neuhofer met me at the AG Farben complex. After a short briefing I was told that from now on I would have to go by the name of Will, in dispatches and in any conversations with other agents. Everyone from Summerall to the other team members had been sent a memorandum that this was to be the new agent's identity.

Amazingly driving on the autobahn was a little like coming home again. The guard at Bad Aibling welcomed me back and phoned the CO, as soon as I entered the base. All of the team members were out to greet me as soon as I parked the car. Summerall was head of the welcoming party with a salute and a handshake.

Summerall said, "Let's all go inside and get this briefing over with before we have a little something to eat, and we have to be on our way to set up camp near the border."

The briefing was indeed short with the bus already packed along with the motorbike. After an early supper and packing the necessary gear from my office, including two pistols with silencers, we were on our way with the first sergeant driving my car. I was instructing him this time while the bus followed closely behind.

I said to the first sergeant, "I know your last name is Belk, what is your first name?"

"It is Jack."

"Alright Jack, as soon as we can, we need to get you a Russian or East German military uniform so you can act as my driver in and around Leipzig."

After parking the car on the Hof Air Base, and being briefed by the quartermaster on border activity, we headed off on the bus to our regular camping area. When the bus driver got to a place that was safely out of hearing distance from the Czech border, Summerall suggested we walk to see if the coast was clear. Snow was falling and lying on the ground, making the trek easier to navigate.

At the border he asked for the night-vision goggles. After a few minutes he motioned for us to start walking back towards the bus. We all were silent until we were on the bus again.

Summerall said, "The forest is full of Soviets, looked like all of them are asleep in their tents. We will have to try another area farther south."

We were on the main highway again going towards Bratislava when the CO went to the folder of survey maps. My suggestion was to turn left just before the town of Arzberg as it would get us close to the border. Also, here the the forest is thick on both sides and would provide cover. I got undressed and put on a Russian uniform from underwear to a Russian tee shirt. The colonel's uniform I was impersonating was taken on one of my assignments last year after he was shot dead. Buck parked the bus when the old man said to stop. We had another short briefing about staying safe. They asked when and where the team should return to pick us up along with the three assets.

I said, "Be here one week from today at this location. If we are delayed, one of us will call you and set up another day. We should be arriving around first light. Do not let the snow be an obstacle as we will be in need of blankets and hot drinks."

We were on our way as they led us into the forest. This time we took the bike out of the bus and walked it to the border area. The first sergeant looked uncertain about his involvement in this assignment.

When we got close to the border, the fence was touching the ground, but the snow helped us see even though it was 10 p.m. They looked through the goggles and patted me and Jack on the back as he motioned for us to go. I took the goggles from him to use on our return. We picked the bike up to take across the barb wire and then pushed it through the trees walking towards the main road.

After an hour of walking we were on the edge of the forest by the tarmac road. We hesitated to see if any lights were visible in the distance. After marking the spot to come back to we got on the motorbike and were now going in the direction of the troops we had seen earlier. After 10 minutes I stopped and told Jack to look through the goggles to see if any bodies were visible. He whispered that there was no one in view, but a vehicle was ahead about 300 yards.

I whispered, "Push the bike ahead of me while I get prepared to deal with any unforeseen problems."

He walked the bike towards the vehicle as I placed silencers on both pistols. The vehicle was similar to one of our three-quarter ton trucks. It was most likely a staff car for a Russian officer. Jack waited at the road as I went to see if anyone was in the vehicle. There was a soldier on the back seat a little larger than the first sergeant. When I opened the back door, he popped up and started to say something just before I shot him in the forehead.

I motioned for the sergeant to bring the bike quickly so we can get the hell out of here. He was shocked to see the dead soldier and started to say something. I put a finger across my lips for him to keep quiet. The key was still in the ignition so we loaded the bike into the back and I took off towards Prague.

Several miles down the road I pulled onto an old farm track and into the trees to dump the body. With the dead soldier on the ground, I ordered the sergeant to strip him even his underwear and put them on him. He was startled and started to protest, I asked if he wanted to stay alive. As he was getting dressed I pulled the nude body into the forest and covered it with limbs and brush.

We were on our way again with the first sergeant driving, while I went through what was going to be his new identity. With a flashlight in the back seat I read his out his new name.

"Your name is Vlad Volgof and you are a lieutenant. Practice your new name and rank in Russian along with your serial number. You are assigned to drive me from now on."

"Wright, what you did was nothing short of murder. Doesn't it upset you taking someone's life from him? I do not want to be part of any criminal acts."

"Look Jack, like it or not, you are now part of this assignment and you will do as you are instructed. I will explain this time why the Russian had to be killed, do not ask me again after an action is done. The soldier will not be found until the spring and will be assumed to have defected.

"It is too late to escort you back to the border. We have to go to a place to rest up and get some sleep, along with food. I will tell you where to drive and if we get stopped you are to speak in Russian only. Stay on this road past the sign to Cheb and in about 30 minutes turn left at the village of Horni Bezdekov with a sign pointing to Hotel Areal Botanika. When we get there, pull up to the garage at the end of the building and drive in when I open the door."

The first sergeant was shaking his head at the prospect of him driving deeper into a Soviet Bloc country. We got to the hotel without seeing any other vehicles on the road. Lenka, a daughter of the owners of who I had a liaison with on a previous assignment, was surprised to see us standing on her front steps.

She kissed me and said, "Oh Billy, it has been so long from the last time you were here. We are full, but your room is ready. Who is your friend, he can stay in your room and you will stay in my room."

"Thank you Lenka, are your parents here?"

"My parents are over at relatives as their room was needed by a Czech general who's staying here. His staff had taken the other rooms. We will feed you in your rooms so the soldiers will not see you."

"Thank you, Lenka. We have a vehicle in your barn and it should have a lock so no one will see it."

The first sergeant was shown to his room with me going in with him to go over an escape plan if this place was compromised. I pointed out his window and told him that once he was in the forest, he or we would be safe from chasing vehicles. It would take three to four days to get back where we crossed over by walking at night, and sleeping during the day in a barn or a lean too with cattle to give out warmth.

We were served breakfast in his room, and afterwards we were able to get some sleep. It was still too early for Lenka to get the other guests up, so she went to her room to draw my bath. As I bathed and got into bed, she slipped out of her robe and asked if I ever thought about the last time we made love.

I said, "Yes, many times."

"Billy, let's talk later, hold me close. Later, you will sleep like a baby."

I couldn't say no and didn't remember going to sleep. It seemed like in no time there was a knock on the door. Turning over to slide out of bed, I noticed it was still dark outside. I felt good and rested. The first sergeant came into to ask if I was going to get up today. He told me it was almost 4 p.m. That was amazing and hard to believe that the time went by so quickly. He wanted to get something to eat, but was afraid to go downstairs as he heard voices coming from the bottom floor.

He said, "She must have worn you out this morning with you not stirring like you normally do."

The only thing I said after that comment was, "I will be out in twenty minutes after I wash and get dressed."

At that moment Lenka came up the stairs with two trays of food and took them to Jack's room. I asked her to unlock the garage as we will be leaving after we eat. She went back downstairs to open the lock and to see to the other guests after she gave me a wink and a giggle.

After we finished our meal, I told Jack to go get the vehicle and wait outside for me. Lenka walked me to the truck wanting to know when I would be back. I told her it could be soon or it could be months.

Back on the road I told Jack that he would have to be careful because of hundreds of bicycles leaving Prague. It wasn't long before we saw hundreds if not thousands of what looked like fireflies. Soon we were surrounded by cyclists going home after a day's work. We pulled into the Gypsy camp and up to my big taxi driving Gypsy's house. He resembled the Jewish actor Topol, so that is the name I called him. He came out to see why a military vehicle was in his drive.

It took Topol a few seconds to recognize who was in a Russian uniform.

He shook his finger and said in broken English, "English, you go too far this time; they kill you slowly when you are taken in chains. You kidnapped driver, maybe you don't need Topol no more."

I assured him that he will always be needed. The rest of his clan came over to see what the commotion was all about. His daughter finally came out to help in interpreting English words he could not speak. After she gave me a really seductive kiss and welcomed me back, she took my hand to lead me inside the house.

Topol wasn't going to let his daughter's exuberance get out of hand.

He said, "English, you are married now, no. My daughter is safe from you."

"No I am not married yet, maybe sometime next year. Yes, your little girl is very safe with me."

He was delighted at my answer and slapped me on the back with his big hairy hand, and then pointed to the kitchen table where we would talk about what was needed. I introduced Jack to everyone, and he wondered why people were looking in the windows from outside the house.

The daughter told him, "Jack, you two are different than our people. Billy or Ludwig is the first Westerner to visit our house. My papa said now you are welcome anytime. Now Ludwig will tell us what is it he wants from us."

I asked the pretty Gypsy daughter to get a piece of paper before we go over the plans. I also needed to know what the cost would be to carry out the job.

"I will need your father to take Jack and me to Bozi Dar tomorrow to see the new construction of a new Russian town. The village of Molivice is next to the proposed town. Tomorrow evening we would like to take the military vehicle to the Gypsy Village outside of Leipzig. I would like your father to meet me at his relative's house in Leipzig on Saturday night. Your father must be well rested as he will be awake all night. Ask him how much it will cost; and one last request, I need $4,000 changed into East German Marks. How many marks will I get?"

While Topol went over the notes with his daughter, I left to hide the military truck in one of the barns.

I told the first sergeant to stay here and answer any questions from the big man.

When I got back, the daughter said her father would like $100 for all of his work. I pulled out a $100 note and thanked him once again for helping me. He told his daughter that the Leipzig Gypsies would get me the marks.

We were fed and I was told to show Jack where my house was as we needed to get some rest.

The next morning after breakfast we went to the new Russian town for the day. There were construction workers all over the area building apartment blocks and large concrete bunkers with soil and grass domed roofs. The first sergeant or Jack walked among the workers asking what was needed as he pointed to me as the procurer of supplies. We learned a lot about why this massive undertaking was going on.

The bunkers were to house nuclear warheads and the apartment blocks were to house lots of military families to keep the Czechs in line and most likely to hide nuclear warheads.

Spending all day at the construction site and eating in a restaurant surrounded by Russian overlords and

Czech workers was a little unnerving to us. We got back to Topol's house just after dark to get the military truck and head off to Leipzig. When we got to the Leipzig camp, the Gypsies came out of their house to see us. It was like an old family reunion with hugs and kisses from men and women alike.

After being fed, Jack and I got on the motorbike to go to my apartment overlooking the guarded old Nazi Base. We stopped at a deli to buy enough food for a week, along with beer and vodka to give away. At the apartment the old landlord came up when I opened my door to see who was upstairs. He was glad to see me and came in for a glass of vodka. I pumped him for information after he finished his first tumbler. Jack was curious how the old man could drink that stuff.

The landlord started talking and really gave us a lot of information. His wife was quizzed weeks ago as to who was living in her building. She told the Stasi it was only relatives and they kept her overnight to see if she was lying. Evidently she never broke and my apartment was never searched. Everything he told me was the best news that could have been heard. He left us with clutching the half full bottle.

I told the sergeant. "When I turn out the lights, open the heavy curtains carefully so we can see the base. If you look over the road, you will see where our assets are kept. You get some sleep while I log all of the activity in and around the gates tonight. I will get some sleep tomorrow as you log who is coming or going through the gates, and when the change of the guards is done."

The first sergeant snored all night helping to keep me from falling asleep. The guards were changed over every two hours, except for the time from 2 a.m. to 6 a.m. That was most beneficial as to know when best we could carry out the extraction.

The sergeant woke up just after the 6 a.m. to change over. When he crawled out of bed, I crawled in and was asleep within seconds. He wanted to talk, but I was out of it and had to get some sleep.I told him we can talk later.

I woke up in the afternoon to find the first sergeant was gone. I was worried and thought the worst like he had turned on the lights and was discovered. After looking out the window to see him walking back across the street toward this place, my feeling of panic subsided at that moment.

When he walked through the door I started in on him. "Are you out of your mind by taking a risk and compromising this operation?"

"Keep your voice down, the lady downstairs is trying to sleep. First, Captain, I watched as an MP came to the gate and hauled the two guards out of the guards' shack. They seemed to be intoxicated and as there were no immediate replacements, I went over to see what was inside of the shack. I slid a window open and climbed inside to get a radio, which may be useful."

"Sergeant that is beautiful; sorry I jumped on you for using your initiative, don't do that again unless you know it is really safe to proceed. Now tell me about your log and the two ladies that visited the guards at 6:30."

"They were dressed in tight pink sweaters and leotard-looking tights. Their hair was teased and rode high above their heads. I reckon they were prostitutes and worked the bars or clubs until this morning. Now, if I was asked why they were wanting to do these guys, I would assume that they were wanting to earn a little extra change before going into the compound to do a couple of the officers inside."

"Fantastic work Sergeant! When you see those two girls again, walk downstairs and see if they would return next Sunday morning at 2:15 to the guard shack."

"I can't speak German; it may raise a red flag."

"Okay sergeant, I will go see the landlord and have him write a note to specify the time and date for them to show up. I will put 50 marks in the envelope and the note will also say another 50 marks will be paid when they have completed doing the two guards. All you have to do is tell the old man when the ladies appear again. I have to go soon and will be back on Saturday evening."

"Where are you going Wright? We haven't had a chance to talk things out. There are a lot of unanswered questions."

"See you sergeant, we will talk when we get back to Bad Aibling."

After visiting with the landlord and making sure the note was written and paying him for another year's rent in advance, I was on the bike headed for Berlin. Everything I needed was on me, two pistols, several passports and lots of cash. What else could a young spy need in a hostile country?

It wasn't long before I was entering the university grounds. There were still lots of bombed out buildings across the street from the entrance.

The war had ended over twenty years ago, and still tons of rubble was piled up. In the office a couple of young ladies came over to help me. After showing them my Cambridge papers and passport, they were surprised that I was German. I explaining to them that I was taken to America by my parents at the age of 10, so my German wasn't as good as my English.

They complimented me with my ability to speak their language as well as I did. They wanted to know if I met Elvis Presley. We started laughing and having a good time talking about living in the South when a dour-looking older lady came out to scold the two students. One of them was up to having a drink at the university club. First, I needed the address of the dorm where the girl who was the head prefect lived, and who was in charge of the reception tomorrow night.

They told me her name is Bianka. She's very bright student, but she was Jewish. After getting her address I gave the one who was going out with me my best Elvis impression, "Thank you, thank you very much!" They were impressed to a point of blushing.

They almost forgot to tell me where my dorm room was. It happened to be in the same building as Bianka's. Now that was a stroke of much needed luck. After putting my bike in the room, I went to a haberdasher to get some decent-looking clothes.

I knocked on Bianka's door and when there was no one in, I left to get cleaned up and get some rest. Helga was waiting outside the admissions office for me with a big smile on her face. She grabbed my hand as we walked around the corner of the building towards the club. I pinned her up against the building and kissed her as I pressed my body against hers. Another young lady walked by going in the opposite direction.

Helga said, "That's the Jewish girl who you were asking about."

I looked towards Bianka as she turned around to see if we were still in an embrace. I smiled at her as she looked embarrassed and quickly turned back around.

When we got to the club I quizzed Helga about why Jewish people are thought of differently. She did elaborate for a long time why they were blamed for Germany's troubles leading up to the war. I gave her my feelings on how so many good people and their children were exterminated, which was too horrific to comprehend.

She did agree and said, "Some people are still hateful towards the Jews, not everyone; however, you are the only one, Ludwig, that I have heard feel compassion for Jews. I like you for feeling that way, at university you must not talk that way because of the communist lecturers vent their hatred for Jews, the English and, of course, Americans in the classrooms."

"Do you fell like going to the Wienerwald for dinner?"

She said, "Der Weinerwald is a quick food place; it tastes good, not healthy though. Students eat there because they give you a lot of fries."

Helga was ready for some food. She looked a little on the thin side. Over dinner she talked about how many tasks she had to do in the university admissions office, including giving out temporary ID cards without having a photo.

We went to her parents' apartment after dinner to introduce me to them. They were interested in information about England, not Cambridge, which seemed a little suspicious. They invited me to stay the night if I needed a place. Helga asked me to stay; she would share her room with me. Now this was a bit unusual as I declined and told them I had to get ready for the other Cambridge students arriving tomorrow morning.

She followed me down the stairs and I asked her if I could see her again. She kissed me this time as my back was to the wall, with her body pressed hard against mine. I had to leave before it was too late to say no.

Back at the university and walking by the club, I spot Bianka in the room stacking chairs. I walked in to see if I could get a conversation going since there was very little time left to get her out of the country.

She accepted my invitation of helping her stack chairs and unfolding old wooden trestle-type tables, which were extremely heavy. Bianka swept and mopped the floor while I arranged the tables again, and put the chairs on one side facing the front of the room. We worked without saying a word for a couple of hours as we surreptitiously looked at each other out of the corner of our eyes.

Finally, we sat down with a glass of wine to admire the job we have done. The place was now ready for the arriving foreign students.

Bianka asked, "When did you arrive Ludwig?"

"This afternoon about 3, why do you ask?"

"You didn't waste time picking up a girl."

"Bianka, I wanted to do Helga a favor for her and her friend being so nice to me and helping me sign in. Helga is a nice, reserved young lady."

She busted out laughing at something and was finding it hard to talk. She did manage to say something like if she is shy then I am the German Chancellor. We both laughed a lot over the course of the evening. Bianka had the look of a bookworm or librarian with long, straight hair and heavy black-rimmed, government-issue glasses. Her skin was as white as flour with a few spots that was hard to ignore. With help she could look stunning as she looked a little like the actress Vivien Leigh.

The evening turned into night without us caring about the time as we enjoyed talking about our past and where we came from. The conversation got around to our views of the world and our philosophy on how we could improve the world we live in. With her pouring another glass of wine, she asked me what I thought about Jewish people.

"I never think of Jewish people, except they got a raw deal in Europe not so long ago just by being Jewish."

"I have no friends here because the other students do not want to be seen with me because I am Jewish."

"How does one know who is of one religion or another religion. You look like some of my relatives."

"Ludwig, you are one of the nicest boys I have met since my childhood and playing with other Jewish children in Leipzig."

"What kind of refreshments and food are going to be served tomorrow at the reception?"

"There is no money provided by the government or the university; I will have some weak coffee here from used grounds. We have wine glasses and beer steins for water. We had the only wine that was available."

"Bianka, I will provide the wine, beer and vodka if you show me where to buy them or have the club serve us drinks. How many students will be here to welcome us?"

"No more than 20 in all, and with your group that number will be a little over 30. Ludwig, it will cost a lot of money for the club to provide the alcohol. Are you sure you could do that?"

"How much will it cost Bianka if we all have three glasses each? You and I will go buy the vodka in the morning and have the club provide everything else, forget about the weak coffee."

"Let's see Ludwig, three marks times 35 is over 100 marks, not counting the vodka."

Bianka was pleased to take the 100 mark note and would tell the bar to stop at that amount. If anyone wanted more, than they could buy it themselves. It was 2 a.m. already as we left to go to our dorms.

I walked Bianka to her room and was about to go to mine when she invited me in to talk some more. She let her hair out of the net like thing, which was keeping it straight and under her hair so it couldn't be seen. That was the strangest-looking hairnet I ever seen.

After about 30 minutes I got up to leave to get some sleep; we were both clumsy from being overly tired and bumped into each other, almost falling over. I caught her and held on until she steadied herself. My arms were around her waist, as I pulled her closer and wanting to kiss her like she had never been kissed before. I had to make a quick impression so she would somehow want us to be more than friends, and perhaps go see her parents together. After we kissed Bianka asked me to stay the night.

Bianka and I fell asleep soon as we were both on the bed, which was all I remembered until we both woke up hours later at the same time in each other's arms. She didn't want to leave my warm body and walk across the cold floor to get ready for the exchange students. She made toast in a little antiquated broiler, with both of us talking about life.

We looked at each other and instinctively knew what each of us was thinking and it wasn't about having toast. Thank goodness we slept late and had little time to do anything else, except clean up the kitchen and get ourselves ready for the party.

Now time wasn't on our side as the noon hour was approaching. The toast was cold and couldn't be reheated as it was already burnt. We barely had enough time to go buy the vodka, get to the hall and turn the heat on. Snow was coming down making the place look a Christmas card with the old university building in the background.

The reception room was ready, still as cold or close to freezing as it was after the heat had been on for half an hour. We both sat down to wait and talk some more.

Bianka asked "Do you like England and America, Ludwig?"

"I love them both equally. It is such a good feeling to know one can be or do anything they like as long as they do not hurt anyone. You feel like a butterfly landing on a beautiful flower or on a green meadow, going wherever you want to go."

"Oh Ludwig, you make it sound so wonderful; and I would like to go with you if it wasn't for my parents having to stay here to work."

"They could find work in England or America."

"You do not understand Ludwig, they tried to leave when I was very young and now they are prisoners, it is so sad."

At that moment the KGB agent from London walked in. He must have been on the students' flight. I muttered *"Oh crap,"* and Bianka asked what was wrong. Hopefully, he thinks I am part of the welcoming committee.

I said, "That man over by the door is a Russian KGB agent and he is one bad man, the students will be here soon."

"How do you know who he is Ludwig?"

"He had attended some of our university meetings. I must tell you something that will happen when my professor gets here. I took the place of a student who couldn't make it, I was the alternate. The student is a good friend of mine. Remember that, because you will ask me questions later on the professor's reaction to me being here."

No sooner had I told Bianka about the coming brouhaha, Rodney walked in with his wife and the Cambridge group behind him. David waved to me and when I waved back the professor saw me. If looks could kill, I would be dead now. He made a beeline straight towards me. I told Bianka to go see that tall dark boy who waved to me. The professor was livid.

63

"What are you doing here? I made it clear you were not wanted on this trip. How did you get here?"

"Now calm down Rodney, you are making a spectacle of yourself. It's not how we play the game ole boy."

The Russian came over to tell him he was wanted at the door and there was a party meeting he had to go to. Rodney was trying to stare me down as his face was getting red with anger.

As soon as the professor was out of the room, Mrs. North came over to add a little salt to my wounds. David and Bianka were watching to see how I handled her. She sat down and said, "Ludwig, tse tse you bad boy, you have a way of not being wanted, would you please get me a vodka and tonic."

While sipping her drink she started in again, "Tell me, why do you agitate poor old Rodders?"

"Jane, I really want him to like me and will do anything for my teacher."

"Ludwig, Ludwig, Ludwig, you are so full of it to a point of being insolent. I want you to leave tonight and don't come back so my husband can do what he came here to do."

"I will leave tonight as soon as we make love; it is written all over your face that you would like to do it with me."

"She got up and gently brushed the back of her gloved hand across the right side of my face, saying as she walked away, "See you tonight, whoever you are."

David came over with Bianka and asked what that was all about with the professor and then his wife.

"He is upset because Leos Novak asked me to take his place as he has some type of flu."

Bianka with a look of incredulous pain on her face said, "You know Leos Novak, why didn't you tell me Ludwig?"

"Keep your voice down Bianka. This trip was a trap, set up by the KGB to take Leos and his girlfriend prisoner so their parents would have to come back to Leipzig and continue working on a secret project."

"Who are you and how do you know all of this."

David said to Bianka, "How could Billy know, I mean Ludwig you knew Leos. I see you two have been up to something in such a short time."

"David, I will need to see you later. Bianka, please sit down and listen to me. Yes, Leos told me he knew you but haven't seen you for a few years. Please, for the safety of Leos, do not discuss this with anyone especially the KGB agent or the professor and his wife."

"Why did he call you Billy, Ludwig? Who are you and what are you doing here if the professor doesn't want you here? I have to get away from you and work out why you seduced me like you did."

Jane was staring at me during the heated spat with Bianka, as David came back over to make amends.

"Sorry about that Billy for letting the cat out of the proverbial bag."

"Maybe it was meant to be as I had to tell her sometime tonight. We will discuss later why you must call me Will back in England from now on. Over here I am Ludwig, don't forget. I will be leaving tomorrow, so cover for me if the professor or his wife wants to know where I am. I have the flu and have been admitted to the city infirmary in downtown Berlin. Since they loathe me, they wouldn't care if I died in there and surely wouldn't visit me."

"It is evident that Bianka is infatuated with you and she may be trouble."

"She is going with me tomorrow if I can talk her into it, and please, that is between us for right now. Cover for her also with the same story. You don't need to know anything else that will get you in trouble."

The evening was dragging on, which allowed me to go to my dorm room to pick up the Russian's pistol and place the silencer on the barrel before sticking it in the back of my trousers. A feeling came over me that the professor was going to get the KGB agent involved in his rage towards me. After all, why wouldn't he?

When I got back I spoke to Bianca and told her how sorry I was to have deceived her. Bianka walked away without saying anything giving the professor's wife the chance to join me.

David, seeing the quandary I was in, went to help Bianka clean up and try to explain what was going on. Jane started in on me again just as her husband walked in with the Russian shadowing him. He came over and told his wife to go talk to someone with a little more class than this fellow.

The Don invited me outside for a confrontation. I walked ahead of him as fast as I could so I could possibly get the upper hand. His wife stopped him and told him he was acting like a fifth grade school boy. I managed to make it across the street and into the shadows of one of the bombed out buildings. As I watched him coming towards me, the KGB agent was about 50 feet behind him. He may be coming to kill me.

When the professor got to me, I raised my left hand to surrender. I had the pistol in the other hand behind my back.

He was about to strike me when I shouted, "Why is the Russian part of our disagreement, sir."

That woke the professor up out of his rage as he turned around and ordered the KGB agent to get back to the reception. The Russian was angry at being spoken to in that fashion. He hit him with a burly right hook as hard as anyone I had ever seen hit before. The professor was out cold before he hit the ground.

The Russian was shouting some gibberish while staring me in the eyes and not noticing I had a gun pointed at his stomach. As I dodged his right hand I pumped three quick bullets into his gut. He crumpled on to the top of the professor. I wiped the gun clean with the back of the Russian's jacket and put it in the professor's left hand.

I ran back as fast as I could so my breathing would be laborious and thus making it look like I was a victim. Collapsing to the floor, one of the local professors hurried over to hear me say that someone had been shot. Everyone ran outside, except Bianka and David, to see who was shot.

David was in back of Bianka when I saw him clap his hands silently and mimed, "good acting." Bianka helped me over to a chair. David was still smiling and suggested she should take me to my room. I gave him a wink to say thank you for that suggestion.

Back in my room, I sat Bianka down and told her who I was and the job I was sent here to do.

"Bianka, you have 10 seconds to tell me yes or no. If you say "yes" you will need to go to your room, and put on clothes that will keep you warm enough while you ride on the back of my motorbike to Leipzig. If you say "no," I will have to leave Berlin soon."

# Chapter 4

## Closing Down the Soviet Base

"Bianka, your parents got word to the CIA through the Novak's that they would like to join their friends in the United States. They would not leave without you. Your parents, Peter and Finja, can be out of their compound tomorrow night, if you want them out of prison. I can then have them go to America. You can also join them, now what will it be, yes or no."

"Yes!"

She started crying uncontrollably. Putting my arms around her shoulders, I told her that she can cry later, and to go get a lot of clothes on. We needed to leave before the police get here. As we were leaving, flashing blue lights could be seen in the distance. Two hours later we were pulling into the Gypsy camp north of Leipzig.

After getting a good night's sleep, we were awakened with breakfast brought over to our chalet. Bianca wanted to know more of my involvement with the CIA.

"When you are in the West, I will tell you more. All you need to know is what you have to do to help your parents escape. It is set up that you will get inside the camp tomorrow night as a cleaning lady. You will tell your parents they cannot take anything with them and to follow you down the stairs to a waiting military truck. There will be a green blanket wadded up on the ground beside the back tire. That is the vehicle you need to get into without saying a word. We will go over this again several times today."

"What do I call you?"

"Ludwig Von Wilhelm is my German name."

The rest of the day we talked only what America was like. Bianka knew I used her so she would want to go with me. I told her all about my girlfriend in London, and we were to be married hopefully within a year. She understood that I love Nicola and there will be no one else outside of her and my ability to perform my job.

We slept the rest of the day so we could be capable of pulling off the extraction in the early hours of the morning. Before it got dark, Bianka helped me load the bike into the military truck. When it was dark we took off for my apartment. As we were leaving

I gave our Gypsy minder a good tip and money for the bike and truck being gassed up.

Once we were in the apartment overlooking the compound gates, we told Bianca that no lights were to be turned on. The sergeant said he took all of the bulbs out just in case we forgot. Bianka asked why we were speaking English and not German. Jack ignored her question and continued on.

He said, "The two lovely ladies were given the money and will be here at 2 a.m. These guards seem to be a little lax in the way they guard the base by drinking and playing a lot of grab ass. Also, while you were gone, the landlady cooked me two meals. It was the best food I've ever eaten; now don't tell my wife that."

"Thank you sergeant, now get some sleep and I will wake you at 1 a.m."

Bianka and I watched to see if she knew anyone going in or coming out of the base. Amazingly no one actually went in or out for three-plus hours. We talked a lot about her parents and the time they almost escaped when the Berlin Wall was being built. By midnight most lights inside the compound were off.

Bianca was still asking questions and asked. "My mother and father were happy for the four friends who were successful in escaping the base last year. Did you have anything to do with them leaving?"

"Bianka, I will tell you when you are in the West; nothing is going to be divulged today, not while you are in a Soviet Bloc country."

She stopped inquiring at that point. I have to watch what I say because of using the wrong word or phrase that may spook her and cause her to change her mind about going through with the extraction. A word like defecting brings into the sphere of one's own nationalistic feelings. Bianka was finally told it was time for her to go downstairs and walk with the landlady to start cleaning the offices and laboratory inside the base.

Bianka was petrified at the thought of going through with the plan and said, "Ludwig, I am terrified that I will be too nervous to do this."

I poured her a large vodka and water to calm her down. That seemed to give her just enough courage to go.

Bianka and the landlady made it inside the compound, and the soldiers began teasing Bianka as she walked through the gate.

It was time to wake up the sergeant to get ready for the scary stuff. The sergeant was getting the jitters and that was making me feel a little nervous. It was way too late for backing out. I poured two large vodkas for me and the sergeant, which seemed to also steady our nerves. I told Jack that no matter what, he was not to say or do anything.

Bianka was already inside and was waiting with her parents. It was now time to give the first sergeant a pep talk.

At the 2 a.m. changeover, the guards were right on time. We were holding our breath waiting for the two prostitutes to show. It was already 2:15 a.m. and they were nowhere in sight.

I built in an extra 15 minutes for a delay such as this. The girls showed up at 2:25 a.m., and it was time for the sergeant to go give them the rest of the money and two bottles of vodka. This time it was topshelf hooch as we didn't need the two soldiers declining a drink because of cheap vodka.

I watched as the delivery was done and the sergeant came back to get me. I kept watching as the two girls were invited into the guard shack while the sergeant was crossing the road.

He opened the door and said, "We now have the ball and it is time to go on the offense Wright."

The bike was pushed to the side of the drive, and we left to try and enter the compound. I was in the back seat with two loaded revolvers with silencers on both barrels. As we pulled up a guard staggered outside, saluted and opened the gate. Bianka was already outside with her parents.

When I got out to let them in Bianka said, "Papa is having second thoughts and his heart is hurting."

I pushed her father in the back seat and took Bianka and her mother to the other side of the vehicle. I made then get inside without saying anything.

I got up front and leaned back to give Mr. Bieber the vodka bottle and said, "Take a few big drinks, which will calm you down and stop your heart from beating so fast."

When we got to the gate a car pulled up wanting to come in.

The sergeant said, "Christ, why does this have to happen now?"

I said, "Pull up to the other gate and we will leave while the guard is distracted."

When he stopped I got out with a pistol poked again in the back of my trousers again. I still had a key to the gate from my last assignment. He drove forward slowly enough for me to jump in.

The sergeant said, "Where in the hell did you get a key to that gate? I can't take any more surprises . What was that other vehicle doing at the gate?"

"That was Topol, coming in at the right time. You didn't see him when we drove in as he was parked on the street waiting for us to start out of the base."

"Thanks a lot Captain for not telling me and having the be Jesus scared out of me. Hell no, I didn't see him."

"Okay, we have two Gypsy scouts staggered one to two miles in front of us, looking for police or military. They will be shadowing us and scouting at the same time until we are in Czechoslovakia. Then we are on our own. Now pull over and follow me as I ride in front of you on the motorcycle."

I could see the other two Gypsy cars pull out onto the road as soon as my cycle lights were on. They were going to travel on the back roads, over the foothills and through two different forests. The snow was coming down hard and covering the road, making the bike hard to keep upright.

An hour later we were crossing into Czechoslovakia and leaving our Gypsy scouts, waving goodbye as we kept motoring. After another hour and a half, we past the area where the soldiers were a week ago, not long now to the new extraction point. It was wonderful to see the large tree limbs over each other. I pulled the bike over by the side of the road and got off. The sergeant pulled behind me and stopped.

I told him, "Keep the engine running while I grab the infrared binoculars from under the front seat."

The coast was clear, no warm body images were seen within a half mile, just a few deer. I placed the goggles strap around my neck and asked for some help in getting the bike inside the truck. We then drove the vehicle into an area in the forest where it would not be seen from the road.

I motioned for the group to follow me, and with the light beginning to shine through the trees it was easy to pick out the trail. As instructed, everyone was walking quietly with the sounds of crunching ice and snow under our feet. When we got to the border and walked across the barb wire laying on the ground, several men appeared that startled the assets. I could see the profile of Summerall. That was a wonderful sight, especially when the staff sergeant appeared from behind a tree. He used to be called Buck for his rank, and he was still called Buck, which sounded better than Staff.

We continued towards the bus as Summerall led the way. When we got to the bus we introduced the team members to the three assets. The three Bieber's were hugging everyone and thanking them all for giving them their freedom.

Summerall shook our hands and even gave the first sergeant a big hug.

As for me he saluted and said, "Well done! I see you brought our first sergeant back safe and sound. By the way, your orders came through the dispatch three days ago on your new rank."

"Thank you, sir. I must go since there is some leftover business to attend to. The first sergeant will fill you in on the operation and he has some extra information on the other matter."

The first sergeant said "Congratulations on becoming a... Wright. I want to say about the incident that first day, it is over. I was out of order and know now that the assignment comes first. When will we see you again?"

"Hopefully before Christmas, I really must hurry and get back to Prague and then on to Berlin."

Bianka came over to hug me and kissed me goodbye as she whispered in my ear, "I will never forget you whatever your name is. I will love you forever." That was bringing tears to my eyes. I had to leave now before the other army members seen me cry.

On the way back to the border I cried like a baby with happy tears streaming down my cheeks. I stopped to rub snow on my face to get me back on track.

My complete concentration was again needed. Stopping about 100 yards from the truck, I thankfully remembered to look through the goggles; you never know what is lurking out there. The coast was clear as I walked on with getting to the truck, and then backing out onto the main road. I abandoned the truck a few kilometers from the new pathway after driving it into the forest on the opposite side of the road. I then took the time to cover it with large limbs. Just maybe I would have to use it another time.

The road to Prague was clear, probably because it was still Sunday morning. I got to the Gypsy flea market to thank Topol for helping me again, and to give him some bonus money. I would need another favor from him in a few days.

The big Gypsy was glad to see me, but not in a Russian uniform. I forgot about my attire. He sent me over to a booth that was selling stolen suits from London and Paris. He also fixed me up with a heavy leather suit, so the bike ride wouldn't be to cold. He invited me to go back with them to the camp; however, I declined since I could be in Berlin before they broke camp here.

I asked him, "What would your charges be to pick me up in Berlin in the taxi and drive three of us back to the Prague Airport on Tuesday morning, and then taking me back to Berlin that same afternoon?"

"English, that is a lot to work out. My daughter wants to see you in the wagon and give you lunch. Now you be good to my little girl; she likes you and keeps asking when you are coming back. I know you have other women, I have seen with my own eyes. Don't break her heart, English."

I climbed into the wagon in the nick of time as two plain clothes police approached Topol's marquee. They looked around and walked towards the wagon. One of them looked inside just after the beautiful Gypsy girl fell on top of me and onto a bed covering me up with her dress. She kissed me for as long as it took for him to go away. After he was gone and out of the tent, she kissed me again and told me to have a seat at a small child like table while smiling and giggling as she made a sandwich. After eating the sandwich, I climbed out of the wagon with her holding onto my neck.

Her large father walked over and said, "English, what did I tell you?"

He let out a big, bellowing laugh when he seen me turn beet root red.

After slapping me on the back he said, "The two trips to Berlin would cost you 1,000 Czech Koruna and for my daughter another 1,000." He let out another large laugh and said, "No English, she is not for sale."

After paying him and saying goodbye to his daughter, I looked back as he counted the money and then letting out another bellowing laugh. His daughter ran after me, and walked me to the area where my bike was hidden behind outside urinals that smelled to high heaven. She kissed me in front of the other Gypsy members without thinking that this couldn't be good for my well-being.

I pulled away from her embrace to say, "Your relatives may not like someone like me messing with one of their young girls."

"They think of you Ludwig as one of us now, especially when my papa says you are part of our family. I could be yours one day Ludwig."

"Leila, what type of guy would I be if I pretended to say you were the only girl I wanted? Besides there may be times I may never come back with my bosses telling me where to go and what to do. Even if I did love you a little, it would be unfair to you."

"I understand Ludwig, I love you also a little."

With both of us laughing at what Leila said, she gave me one last kiss before riding out and following the river towards town and the road to Berlin.

When I got back to my dorm room, a note was on the bed telling me what room David was in.

I knocked on his door; he was white as a sheet when he finally opened the door.

"What is wrong? You look your coming down with something."

"Billy, I mean Will, I haven't been able to get any sleep with the police taking me to their headquarters every night since the reception. Professor North was held for two days and tortured while being accused of murdering the KGB agent with his own gun."

"Where have you been since last Friday night? The Stasi are looking for you and the young Jewish girl. You better get away before someone tells them you were seen. I don't know what they did to North; he can hardly walk. Why would you come back when you knew the man was murdered and probably by you."

"I came back to get you and the North's out of here. Get your plane ticket, passport and money, we are leaving now. Put on all of your clothes so you will stay warm; put all of your socks on your feet."

"Will, the police have everything, even my money. Where are we going?"

"To a Gypsy camp, where the police cannot find you."

We left on the bike just as a car pulled into the university. I had barely enough petrol to get to Topol's village. Good thing it was this side of Prague. When we arrived, Topol came out of his house to see what was wrong; he knew it was me as no one else he knows has a motorbike. He helped to get David inside and sat him at the table with the wife bringing us both a bowl of hot soup.

David was now safe and I had to get back to Berlin to get the professor and his wife. Leila showed David to my chalet after consuming all of the soup.

I told David, "You need to get some sleep. I will be back soon to get you, now don't answer the door or go outside of this house."

Topol and I left in the taxi to go back to Berlin and to get the two North's. We got to the university dorm at 3 a.m. I knocked on the professor's door with Jane saying, "Go away, do not bother us again, we are so tired of you people."

"Jane, open the door, I have come to help you; it's Ludwig."

"Ludwig, what are you doing here, everyone is looking for you. Where have you been?"

"Listen carefully, throw your stuff in a suitcase, we have to leave now. You can get dressed in the taxi."

"My husband is too weak to walk very far."

I picked up the thin, small professor and started carrying him out of the door. I told Jane to get her clothes and follow me now, no more talking. We were on our way as they both got dressed as well as they could. Topol knew to go to Prague Airport.

We arrived at the airport just before seven and had to hurry to catch the BEA flight that left at 7. I ran inside to the counter and gave the ticket agent the North's passports that I had stolen a few weeks earlier. I told the ticket agent Professor North was very ill, and needed two first-class seats to London. After paying with Czech cash, I went back with the tickets to help Topol get the two of them to the gate as they were holding the flight for the two first-class passengers. At the gate I picked up Mr. North and carried him in my arms up the steps. When I sat him in his seat, the flight engineer came back to see what all of the fuss was about.

I whispered in his ear, "I work for her Majesty's Secret Service. If you get a radio message for your flight to return to the airport, make a crackling noise into the microphone as if there is static in the area. Whatever happens, do not turn back. Radio ahead for an ambulance and tell your operations manager to contact MI 5."

I turned to Jane and told her they would be home soon after handing her their passports and ticket stubs. She looked confused.

She started crying and asked, "How did you happen to have our papers? Who are you?"

As soon as I walked down the mobile steps the plane door closed and the two engines were already running. Topol and I went to the parking lot until the plane was airborne. He then drove us back to the Gypsy enclave where I found David fast asleep. The time was now 9 a.m. and we would have to wait until dark to take off for the border. I made a bed on the floor and slept until I heard David get out of bed about 3 p.m.

David and I went to Topol's house to tell him we were leaving as soon as it got dark. He told us it would be better if we left a little before so we could see if any roadblocks were set up. The bike was gassed and ready to go.

I said, "If we leave now we would be hitting the rush hour around Prague since our route takes us through the outskirts of the city."

The big Gypsy said, "That is good, the police stay away at that time."

We were given a small flashlight to use in the forest. After getting through the hordes of cyclists, we were on the road to Cheb and the border. When we got to Horni Bezdekov it was now getting dark and a roadblock could be seen with several vehicle lights shining in the dark. I turned at the sign to the Areal Botanika Hotel.

When we stopped I told David, "Open the garage doors so we can hide the bike in case the police or army guys had seen us turn off. Let's hurry and go inside the hotel before someone comes."

Lenka came out when she heard the large heavy door open. She kissed me like she hadn't seen me for years. At that moment a military truck pulled up to the front of the hotel with two men getting out.

Lenka said, "Your room is unlocked; go in there and stay in the bathroom until they leave."

In the bathroom David wanted to whisper something. I put my index finger over my lips to signal that there will be no talking. We were in there for over an hour before Lenka came to say everything was good.

Lenka told the Russian and the Czech officer, "There is a teenage boy who takes his motorcycle into the forest to run down the trails. I didn't think he came from our village. Now, Billy, are you staying the night again? Where is the other man you brought with you last week? You can stay in my room again."

"No Lenka, we have to go if the roadblock is gone, which will be soon if that was the same army truck used for the checkpoint."

"I have some food on the stove for you to eat, and then while you are eating I will go see if the men are gone."

David asked, "How am I getting back to England without a passport and more importantly, how are we going to get past a guarded border? You have people all over the place helping you, not to mention the young ladies who seem to need your attention. This trip is beyond my comprehension on how to cope in a place where everyone is being watched most of the time. How do you have so many people wanting to help you? It is mind-boggling."

Lenka came in to tell us the roadblock was now gone. After gulping down a bowl of soup and telling our host goodbye, we left to get on the motorcycle. It felt good to be on the road again going home.

As we were getting close to the place to walk towards the border, I backed off the bike's throttle so I could listen if anyone was in the trees. After coasting close to half a mile slightly downhill, I spotted the marker.

I stopped to look through the goggles to see if anyone was in front of us. It was clear in front, but to the right by about 100 yards there was a bunch of soldiers. They had to have heard me unless they were busy talking to each other.

I whispered to David, "We have to walk quickly and quietly. Follow me; you push the bike while I keep looking to see if anyone is getting close."

The soldiers were heading our way and would intersect us if we didn't go any faster. It was no use they had torches and were too spread out for us to go around, we would have to hope they passed by us.

There were foxholes or where wild boars dug into the snow, which would shield us from view.

"Quietly help me pull the two big limbs on top of that small hole. We will quickly place the bike on top of the limbs. Now cover the bike with brush and small limbs. Now help me pull two more large limbs over all of that. Crawl under the other side, and do not breathe through your nose only your mouth very quietly," I whispered to David.

David had to be feeling the freezing damp tundra-type ground; good thing he had an extra set of clothes on, and I had the thick leather suit. Within 20 minutes we could hear the soldiers talking and walking all around us. It must have been an hour before they couldn't be heard any more. I quietly told him to stay put no matter what happens, while I pulled a pistol out of its holster and the silencer from inside my coat pocket. With the pistol in one hand and the goggles in the other, I wormed out of the hole. I popped my head up first to see if anything or anyone was close-by. A deer was next to our den, which meant no one was around. I looked through the goggles and saw the troop of soldiers were over 100 yards from us and going away.

"Okay David, it is time to go. Let's get the bike out."

We quietly uncovered the bike as I had another look through the infra- red goggles. Thank God no one could be seen. We were on our way again and after almost an hour we were at the border. I looked through the glasses and saw four or five men lying on the ground, probably in tents.

I told David, "Look through the glasses; I will have to go see who they are. Stay behind that large tree. Don't move for any reason."

With the pistol cocked I got close enough to hear the first sergeant talking to the old man. I turned around and went to get David.

David asked, "Who are the people up in front of us?"

"They are part of my team."

"What do you mean? Are you part of another team over here?"

David and I walked into the middle of their camp scaring them all to hell.

The first sergeant said, "Christ almighty, Wright, you scared the crap out of us. We could have been East Germans you crazy SOB!"

"I was here 30 minutes ago listening to you tell the old man how much you loved me."

"You are going to get a good ass whipping when we get you back to headquarters and the boys will hold you down while I do it."

By this time everyone was laughing and didn't notice David.

Summerall asked when he finally saw him, "Who in the hell is that guy? And what is he doing here with you?"

"It's a long story sir, can I tell you on the bus. You do know you have camped in enemy territory, and there is a troop of Czech and Russian soldiers just over that far hill, sir."

"The hell you say, I thought we were still in West Germany. Anyway let's go get something to eat. Are you able to drive your car home without falling asleep or should Buck drive it?"

"Buck better drive, we have had a rough time of it."

When we were on the bus going to Hof Air Force Base to pick up the car, so I had time to ask, "How did you know we were coming in this evening?"

Summerall said, "A British Airline pilot called British security services to say two assets in rough shape were landing at Heathrow Airport, and to have MI5 call General Simpson to let him know one of the Queen's own agents was on the move behind the Iron Curtain. At least that was what the pilot was told to say to London. Simpson was wondering what does that have to do with the CIA, and he put two and two together and came up with the Wright summation. You introduced David to us, tell us about him."

"David is a CIA operative working out of London; and that is all I know about him at this time."

David quickly interjected, "I'm a low-level CIA agent."

I added, "Not after this trip, you are as operational as any of us."

We were going through the Hof Base gates as the MPs shined their flashlight into the bus.

David was startled at what he was witnessing and asked, "What is this place that has to have guard dogs and security forces?"

No one answered David for security reasons; Buck found the keys on top of the left rear tire.

On the way back, David had an old wool Army blanket around him as he slept on the floor. The rest of us crowded up front to talk over what kind of successes were accomplished during the last few weeks. The first sergeant had us laughing with tales of hookers, Gypsies and having the crap scared out of him when a car drove up to the Stasi-guarded base. He talked without divulging secrets about the mission. He did say his days of sneaking into communist territories were over; he was getting too old for that kind of work. I excused myself to go to the rear of the bus to sleep.

We were awakened when the bus parked outside the sleeping quarters and were told to get some sleep. The briefing will be held after a late breakfast, and then we could leave for the Frankfurt Airport to catch the 6 p.m. flight to Heathrow.

The first sergeant told us General Neuhofer was en route and wanted to be here for the briefing. At that moment Neuhofer walked into the briefing room and told us to stay seated as Summerall attempted to call us to attention.

He said, "Wright, take the podium, you will go first. Now we do not have time to elaborate on trivial details or when you had to buy anyone off or how much money you spent on gasoline or anything else. I have to be back in Frankfurt by 5 p.m. and so do you. If you please, proceed.

With making sure the tapes were running I said, "After the first sergeant and I crossed the border I managed to commandeer a Czech military light staff truck. We would use this vehicle to extract the three assets from their secure base."

After going into the obstacles of fleeing Berlin and freeing the people involved, I continued on for a further couple of minutes.

"The professor and his wife were put on a flight to London yesterday while David and I made our way to the border. We successfully crossed late last night and are here to talk about it. That is about all there is to say for now."

David was asked to sum up his part of the operation. He looked a little overwhelmed to be talking in front of an American general.

Finally he said, "Excuse me for disagreeing with Will. It wasn't anywhere near as easy as that. We barely evaded the Berlin authorities and ended up surrounded by a large concentration of troops and rode on a motor cycle in subzero temperatures for over six hours. It was a miracle we are alive to talk about it. I will never go on another trip like the one I was on."

The first sergeant was next and said, "I agree with David. It wasn't a simple in and out operation. There is a network of people in the Czech Republic and in East Germany that is loyal to agent Wright. Without them, it would have been much less safe and I for one would have been in some gulag by now. I chastised Wright in the first couple of hours for being so heartless and a cold-blooded killer. As I went further into the assignment I saw just how focused he became. He appreciated his helpers, with treating them in a professional manner.

"In closing, I would like to say something if I can do it without crying. Thank you, Wright, for bringing me home; and please forgive me for wanting to quit in the first few hours. I never can go on another covert assignment; I am not made of the same material as you. I pity the poor slobs who are stalked by this man. He will stop at nothing to achieve picking up or delivering his assets."

The general got up to the podium, blew his nose and said with a crackly voice, "We need to go. I want to know all of the sordid details of what the secret police did to David on the way back to Frankfurt."

One of the MP's was told to drive my car with David and me sitting in the back seat alongside General Neuhofer to go over the trivial stuff. When the general went into Summerall's office for a private conference, we walked outside to wait by the green Army sedan.

I told David, "I do not want to be trapped in a car with Neuhofer for four hours. I would much rather drive myself. Let him do all the talking and we do all the listening."

Leaving the base and before we pulled through the gates, Neuhofer started in on his early Army days when mules were the main cargo carriers. We acted interested for the four hours. The general started in about the Cold War as we pulled up to the airport.

At the airport curbside I said, "General, David's passport was taken off him by the German police."

"Let him use one of your passports, they never look at the photographs anyway. What name will he be traveling under?"

"Ludwig Von Wilhelm."

"I will go in with you to make sure he is allowed to go; I have to allocate and validate your tickets anyway. David, we will have another briefing and I will finish my stories. Wright already knows all of my past experiences."

At the counter a young female ticket agent asked the general what class of service. I threw my voice with a deep-sounding harrumph and said, "Two first-class tickets, if you please."

She said, "Yes sir, names please."

The general was not amused as he said, "First class, what insolence."

## *Chapter 5*

## Capitulation of a Cambridge Don

We were boarded early and asked what drink we would like. The pretty ticket agent ran on board and gave me a note. It smelled of perfume; I opened the note and read that she would like to show me the sites of Frankfurt the next time I was in Frankfurt, along with her phone number. I stuffed the note into the seat pouch in front of me.

David was taken aback by how friendly European ladies were. I concurred and told him they all seem to have a good work ethic. We laughed and kidded each other almost all of our way to London.

When we arrived without any luggage, we were out of the terminal in a jiffy when someone yelled, "Oy, oer ere, Guv." It was Kenny.

"Where's your totes, Guv?"

"We have no luggage; it was taken away by some really bad boys."

"I believe you, Guv. Sheep country is it boys."

"Yes Kenny, sheep country. Tell me about the ambassador, has he been a naughty boy again?"

"No Guv, and the Russian geezer ain't been seen 'ere eever, since you turned is place over."

David looked at me in the back seat of the taxi as to say, you didn't.

"I know Kenny, he was shot and killed in Berlin."

"With 'is own gun I suspect, Guv."

"Yes, unfortunately, it went off by mistake."

With Kenny chuckling and mumbling like he thought so, David turned to me and asked, "How would Kenny know he was shot by his own gun?"

Kenny was looking at us in his rear view mirror. I nudged David for him to look at the mirror.

Kenny muttered, "I let the cat out of the bag again, ave I Guv."

We all were seeing the funny side to the quips of our taxi driver.

David said, "You are one scary bloke, mate; I think the sergeant was right when he said you were one cold SOB."

We were dropped at my flat at precisely 9 p.m. We said goodbye to Kenny and hello to Leos and Monika when they appeared out on the pavement. They wanted to know why we were back so soon. They told us about the professor being transferred from a London hospital to Addenbrookes Hospital. He has internal injuries that resulted in an emergency surgery here in the teaching hospital. He is recovering, but still not out of the woods yet. The professor had contusions to the kidneys and a perforated liver. He must have been in some kind of horrific accident.

After we went inside Monika put the kettle on. The two friends wanted to know about the accident. We all sat at the table for the briefing to be given to these two young agents.

David started with, "The professor had no accident; he was interrogated and tortured by the Stasi in Berlin. I was taken in for questioning, with them confiscating my passport; and with the truncheons the police had in their hands, I would guess he was hit quite a few times. They didn't keep me long as I wasn't a witness to the murder of a KGB agent. At that time they did not question me on Will's whereabouts."

101

Monika asked, "How was the professor in the area of a murder? And if the police had your passport, how did you get back to Britain? And who is Will?"

David replied to her, "Will is Billy; Billy has been mentioned too many times in dispatches, so the ASA in Frankfurt said he had to be known from now on as Will. The professor was in a fistfight with Will in a bombed out building across the street from where the welcoming party was. The Russian followed them, strangely he was the same one stationed in London. He's the same one who had attended meetings here at the university. The man was the only one unable to walk out of those ruins. Will left the area and Berlin on his motorcycle with a student called Bianka."

Leos wanted to know, "Was it Malenkov, David? Billy had a girlfriend in Berlin, where could they escape to?"

"Yes, it was the man who went on the trip and the girl was one of the three people Billy, or I mean Will, had to bring across the Czech border. They ended up going to Will's flat in Leipzig, and from what I would guess went over the border soon after that. He was back in Berlin within a couple of days to get me and the North's out of Berlin. The North's were flown out of Prague and I was taken into West Germany. The whole ordeal was not for the nervous. I couldn't go through that again. I really don't know if it was Malenkov."

I was comfortable having David give information to Leos and Monika or a briefing so my explanation couldn't come back to haunt me at a later date, when it may be a Will said or David said type of question. I got up to make another pot of tea, and let the three of them hash it out. They didn't even notice me leaving the table.

I finally did join in by asking who wanted tea, and looked over to see three hands in the air without them turning around acknowledging the efforts of the tea man. They were enthralled with David's tale of going covert in East Germany.

Leos said, "I never would go over there with Will or anyone to help someone escape or defect. There are so many questions, David, that I am sure Will would not tell us about the close calls. I remember when he brought me over he was taken prisoner by three soldiers at a roadblock. He caught up with our taxi within 10 minutes with the soldiers' truck and no soldier in sight."

"I never heard that story, Leos. What do you think happened to the three soldiers? I am sure from my experiences this past week they probably didn't need a doctor. More like a shovel."

Monika turned around to look at me as I was leaning against the sink listening to the guys' war stories.

She asked, "Billy, what did happen between you, the professor and Mr. Malenkov in that building?"

"Okay, Monika that is the only question I am going to answer before being debriefed in Simpson's office in the embassy. The Russian wanted to question me on my identity. The professor was in a rage and wanted to smash my face in. They got into a wrestling-type tussle where the Russian ended up shot with his own gun and was killed. Now if you guys excuse me, I have to go see how the professor is getting on."

"One more question Billy. You, in the past, have been quite descriptive but not this time. You never said he pulled his gun out of a holster or his coat pocket. Was it because he never had the gun on him?"

"I have to go Monika, and that was two questions. You should think about being a lawyer. All of you remember from now on and this very important. What is said in this room stays in here, and no one must hear about your experiences. I expect a phone call from Simpson and Thibodeau today. Take down the time, date and where I have to be, in London or wherever they want me. I will be back in about two hours."

Leos was puzzled as to why I would help the professor since he never cared for me being at Cambridge University. I ignored him and was on my way out.

David wanted to go with me to see the North's and pick up some flowers for his room. I left after taking the last sip of tea.

At the hospital there were students sitting on the stairs leading to the professor's room, which was actually a ward that resembled something out of a war movie. It was useless to try to speak to him with so many others patients a foot or two away. He seemed to be asleep anyway.

As I was walking out of the building his wife Jane bumped into me. She wanted to get some answers that were bothering her and the professor as they had time to think what just happened to them. I brushed her off and said the chancellor wanted to see me. Of course, that was a pork pie as the Cockneys would call a "lie."

I went to see the vicar at the university instead of going back to a flat with inquisitive associates, which was not a good thing. The vicar and I talked in confidence about the professor and his attitude right now. I figured he probably had visited Rodney a couple of times to give him some type of spiritual guidance.

The vicar gave me lots of needed information in a surreptitious way that probably seemed to him was not divulging a private matter between him and the professor.

In a deliberate, quiet and soft manner he said, "Rodney (as the vicar called him) was not the same person that left a week or so ago as the one who returned. It is like someone had transformed him into a different being. No one knows what road he would like to travel on now; do you know what I mean Ludwig?"

"Yes, Vicar, I do know exactly what you mean. He has had a life- changing incident and has found out a truth that he had ignored for decades."

"Exactly. Now how do you know what had happened to cause such a transformation in Berlin? Were you there?"

"Yes sir, I was smack dab in the middle; however, I must not elaborate on the professor's state of mind before he went or after."

"He has said that he was so wrong about your character, and his words, not about your presence. What do you think he meant by saying, not your presence. He seemed to, I don't know, say things are not always as it seems."

"I have an idea what has caused his transformation. Now what about his wife, has she also seen the light, sort of speaking?"

"Oh no, my dear Jane still thinks what I say is a lot of mumbo jumbo. Jane seems to be agitated that Rodney has become a much more caring person, and blames it on being bumped on the head. I must go Rodney, I mean Ludwig, the missus will have tea ready."

David saw me come out of the chapel and was looking all over town for me. The general had called; we both have to be in Brighton on Saturday night and you would know where to meet him. Also, our girlfriends are invited. We went to the university club for a beer. It was good to be safely back in England as we both agreed. Leos and Monika walked in to see if they could join us. Everyone agreed to discuss all of our Christmas plans and not the trip in this place.

Within an hour the professor's wife came in and stridently walked over to me and shouted in my face, "I want to see you outside now, whoever you are, you bloody impostor."

"No Mrs. North, I will see you tomorrow morning at the hospital cafeteria."

She walked just as rigidly back out and stopped at the door to give me the finger. I ignored her and thought to myself *we didn't say a time.* Oh well. I also asked no one to laugh at her gesture as that would agitate her even more. She has been through a lot of trauma recently. Everyone in the bar was looking at one us wondering who the impostor was.

The next morning I was in the hospital early enough to see the vicar do his rounds as he thought I was there to see how Rodney was doing. Jane was already in the ward arguing with Rodney; being curious, I stopped to visit with an old man who was asleep two beds down. My back was to the North's and the conversation coming from her was loud enough for the whole ward to hear. She was telling him to snap out of it and come to his senses, and stop the nonsense of saying Ludwig saved his life. He mumbles something making her to leave in a huff.

I went over to his bed and said, "It is good to see you over here and getting the medical attention you need. I am sure if you were still in one of the communist gulags you would not survive any more beatings."

He started to sob and tried to talk.

I said, "Please, do not cause any more stress to yourself. I will come and see you tomorrow."

He smiled and shook his head. As I was leaving the ward the Vicar came in and wanted to know how Rodney was feeling.

I told him I was on my way to keep an appointment and would like to stop by his office this afternoon. He was alright with that; now to see what Jane wanted.

The professor's wife was waiting for me to show with a scowl on her once pretty little face.

Her opening remark as I sat down was, "I hope you were not up stairs visiting my husband."

"In fact, I did stop by his ward along with the vicar."

"What on earth were you doing with that old fool and who told you that you could visit the professor? I want some answers from you right now on your reason for having our passports. They were taken from our house the day before the trip."

"I took them out of Malenkov's jacket pocket. Now think back to the time they were stolen, did the Russian leave the going away party early and why do you think he had to leave? He knew you and your husband were going to be out of the house for a few hours. If you were burgled, how did they get in and did they leave a clue as to who broke the door or window to gain access?"

"My stupid husband left the loo window open and the perpetrator came through the bloody window. Why would you go through someone's pockets that was evidently shot and killed?"

"He wasn't going to be needing the money in his pockets, the bent secret police would have relieved him of anything valuable anyway, so why not me?

Of all the luck the ring on his left pinky finger wouldn't budge."

"You are without doubt the lowest of the low. We are curious how you were able to sneak into Eastern Europe without special permission, and show up at the reception; and for that matter, how did you get out of the country?"

"Jane, my darling, if you agree to meet me this Sunday morning at 11 a.m. inside the university chapel, I will then and only then answer your questions. We are going to church you and I. Sit in the first row on the right side. Do not turn around to see if you can see me. I don't want the congregation to know we have a prearranged date. I will be a few minutes late to make it look as if I sat down to get out of everyone's line of vision."

"I have never stepped inside of that place; however, I will, just to get some answers. I am doing an investigation into your activities from when you first set foot in Cambridge."

"Thank you for warning me. You do have a reputation of being one of the most fair, compassionate, and very attractive ladies in Cambridge. I have to go now, see you in church."

It was barely time to be get to my second class; the first class has been canceled until next year.

As I walked in the lecturer stared at me and said, "I thought you went back to your own country since we haven't seen you for the last 10 days Herr Von Wilhelm. Can you explain your absence, sir?"

"Yes sir. I was an alternate on the exchange students group and traveled to Berlin with my friends. Some of us returned to assist the North's in getting back safely. He is in the local hospital, sir, as we speak."

"I know where he is you bloody insolent Nazi. I know you were not asked to go on that particular trip, what do you say about that?"

"It is too complicated to go into right now, sir. The length of your class would be easily used up in our personal banter. Professor North will be able to alleviate your fears of me being truant, sir."

"Get out and never come back in my class, do you understand."

"Yes, I think I do, sir."

David stood up and said, "You have no right to treat one of these students like that! Your prejudices are nauseating, he is not a Nazi, we all can attest to that. If he goes, the whole class will follow. Do you want to test us, sir?"

"Alright, have it your way, you're all a bunch of collaborators."

At that the class walked out, except one person of royalty, and his security officer. We all went to the university pub for a drink before lunch. While we were in the lounge the chancellor came in to apologize for the professor's actions, and told us we all would be compensated if we returned tomorrow. He told us he will be taking over the second class lecture until a replacement was found. He then bought a round of drinks, and told us to take the rest of the week off and we would still be counted as present. The chancellor sat next to David and myself, and told us how he appreciated our heroic efforts in getting Professor North back home.

The rest of the class wanted to know about the trip and its difficulties. The chancellor mentioned that a special assembly will be organized to commemorate Ludwig and David as soon as the lecturer was fit enough to attend. He then headed back to his office.

David and I stopped at the chapel to see the vicar as prearranged. He was happy to see us and had his wife bring us all a cup of tea.

I asked him, "Do you have a sermon in mind for this Sunday?"

"Yes, I am working on one at the moment; it is still in the early stages."

"Is that a no then Vicar?"

"You are an astute young man Ludwig, why do you ask?"

"Would a short sermon on Jezebel be possible? The right honorable Mrs. North has been persuaded to be in church vicar. She cares for the well- being of animals, but not her fellow man."

"Yes, I think I have a sermon in mind. Daniel in the lion's den may do the trick. Jezebel may be a little harsh."

"Make sure the lions are treated well."

The Vicar let out a large laugh and quickly put his hand over his mouth to muffle the laughter. David and I left after drinking our tea and headed to the flat. We had the rest of the day off, and after leaving our books at the flat we went to see our friend Burt who ran the punts on the river Cam.

Back at the flat, Leos was having a sandwich and said they heard what happened in our second class. It was all over the school when the chancellor went into the almost empty classroom and asked the lecturer to clear out his desk.

Monika wanted to know how I was able to stay focused and not be embarrassed in front of my classmates.

Friday afternoon was here with David, his girlfriend and me being picked up by Kenny. We went to get Nicola in Harrow as she came out of school, and then continued on to Brighton for the weekend.

Nicola looked happy as she was walking across the school's parking lot, and with some of her boys in dark green uniforms already taking off their straw hats. She did a loud throat clearing, making the boys turn around and one of them saying, "Sorry Miss, it won't happen again."

Kenny said, "Now that's a load o toffs and tuffs for ya, afternoon Miss Nicola ave a nice day ave ya,

I got your Guv and some of is friends with im, fancy a trip to the grand on Brighton Beach?"

"Oh how wonderful Kenny; hello darling, I would love to go. I have to go home and change my clothes, my bag is already packed. I knew you wouldn't tell me when you were arriving. Hi David, I haven't met your lady friend."

Four hours later we were all in the posh public lounge as the three generals walked in with their wives, who joined us for a drink before dinner. The three wives were dressed in long gowns and the generals in attractive wool, pinstriped suits. They didn't mind that we were presentable, but definitely not dressed as nice as those three couples.

General Simpson had arranged earlier that a table for 10 be provided somewhere in the back of the dining hall. We all enjoyed each other's company and agreed not to talk shop. David and I were quietly asked to be in the breakfast room at 7 a.m. Before retiring for the night, General Thibodeau asked everyone else if it would be alright if we meet at 9 a.m. for breakfast.

The next morning David and I went down at 6:50 a.m. so we wouldn't be late. With the breakfast hall being closed and dimly lit, a waiter saw us walk up and came out to take us to where the generals were having their coffee. I should have known they would have had everything organized and also be early.

General Neuhofer started the briefing by saying, "Thank you Will, thank you David for agreeing to meet us here in Brighton for the debriefing. I have briefed the generals on the assignment from your earlier reports while we were all in Bad Aibling last week. We all concur it was a great success, but are puzzled over one part of your operation. It was unfortunate a Russian agent was killed and two of our agents left Berlin without telling the authorities. The secret police think that a Rodney Chesterton North and a David Chesterfield are CIA operatives."

One agent called Ludwig was never interrogated as we were told he left earlier with a female student. David, how and why is North involved?"

"Sorry general, I have no idea and never asked why or was never given the reason why."

"Wright, please enlighten us."

"I will go over everything that wasn't in the report from start to finish. The day before going to Bad Aibling, someone burgled the KGB agent's flat in London and coincidentally the home of Professor

North's was also burgled. These victims were all at the same bon voyage gathering going over their itinerary while in East Berlin. Certain documents found their way into my possession."

General Thibodeau jumped in before I continued by asking, "Sorry to interrupt you, but explain what documents?"

"They are the same documents that you have in Washington, plus two British passports, a Russian pistol and 5,000 British pounds."

"Continue."

"The next day I arrived in West Germany with the contraband that was to be used in our operation."

"In Berlin, at a reception, the KGB agent was killed with his own gun and it was made to look like the professor did the dirty deed."

General Thibodeau then asked, "Was all of this premeditated?"

"After the burglaries, sir, a plan was borne to include the professor's passports."

General Simpson was curious as he is head of CIA operations in Europe, and asked, "You think you'll get this professor to work for us?"

"No sir. He would never work for the Americans. I think he can be transformed into an anti-communist propagandist, thereby helping us to stop future sleeper cells here in Cambridge."

"The professor has three weaknesses:He likes young female friends. He tolerates his wife even though she is a harsh protagonist of her own agenda most of the time. His third weakness is he will take the opposite side to any suggestion because he thinks of himself as a more intelligent being than anyone. If he can be turned, my services will no longer be needed here and I can get on to the next problem, which is our own ambassador in London."

"How close is he to being transformed and will his wife undo the transformation?"

"He is a week away from seeing the light. The transformation of his wife is starting this Sunday morning in church."

General Thibodeau was intrigued by this topic as he asked disbelievingly, "How can you work on her when you are not going to be there and probably won't get back until Monday?"

"A higher power than me will be invading her thoughts. She does not care for me or my being at Cambridge. She is working to get me expelled from the campus. No, not me; God will be her inspiration. You see David and I had a talk with the vicar a few days ago and since she has the same feelings for him to put it mildly he is preparing a special sermon for her. She is being tricked in going to church for the first time in decades or maybe this will be her first visit ever."

Thibodeau, with his elbows on the table leaning over closer to me, asked, "How can one be tricked into going to a church service?"

"Mrs. North likes to be in charge of any puzzle, with not being in possession of all the pieces she finds it hard to settle. I have the missing information on what really happened to her husband in Berlin. I told her the only way I could meet her to provide the missing pieces was in the church pew this Sunday."

At that moment the three ladies walked in. We all couldn't believe it was 9 a.m. already. The generals suggested we get back together this evening for an hour before dinner.

After breakfast Nicola and I excused ourselves to have a walk on the beach. David and his girlfriend joined us with the girls asking us not to talk business as they wanted a relaxing stroll to walk off the breakfast, even if it was cold with the icy wind coming off the British Channel.

When we got back to the hotel, David and I went into the lounge for a pint of beer. General Thibodeau noticed us at the bar; I barely had enough time to order him a triple Scotch and soda on the side.

He was about to call the bar man when David said, "Sir. I believe Will has a drink coming for you."

As he was handed his drink he said, "Ah, just what the doctor ordered, Wright let me know if mother walks by."

David and I laughed as he gulped down half of the drink quickly and then added a little soda. Our girlfriends walked in with Nicola ordering what the general was drinking, and David's girlfriend having an Old Etonian. I pulled out my wallet when the bar man said, "Sorry sir, the tab is already spoken for."

Thibodeau asked the barman, "What is that Etonian drink young man?"

The barman said, "It is two dashes of creme de noyaux with crushed ice, shaken, not stirred."

"Thank you, it looks good. You know, Wright, I do like your choice of friends, and both mother and I do look forward to these weekend getaways. We are looking forward to seeing you and Nicola on Sasparilla Island in the new year."

"Gasparilla Island, sir. It's a place to go to relax and fish."

"I better go before I am found down here. See you and David this afternoon."

That afternoon the girls showed the three generals' wives where the famous lanes were, a good place to shop for souvenirs and antiques. I wanted to go see if anyone was fishing in the surf.

David and I were downstairs in the lounge when the three generals came down to get the briefing started. We all ordered a pint of beer and headed to an empty area of the lounge.

# Chapter 6

## London's American Embassy is Compromised

Thibodeau started the briefing by asking, "Wright, what is the time frame for ceasing operations in Cambridge?"

"By the end of the school year, sir."

"Good, we have two other covert actions that have to be started this year. First, you will go covertly into black ops in London with renting a place where you or David can set up a surveillance point to watch the area where the ambassador normally goes to meet the KGB agents. I believe you know the area you need to watch. The budget will be handled out of Washington with a checking account in the name of the operation called Anglo American minerals. I would like for you two with your girlfriends to start looking for a flat tomorrow," Thibodeau added.

"The second operation concerns the new Russian city being built in the Czech Republic. Work on that assignment mentally and be ready to go by this coming Easter semester. Keep using your student status as cover. The Czech operation will be on the back burner and you will not be asked about it until March. The ladies are now here; let's go out to greet them. We will talk again on a Florida beach. General Simpson will keep me up-to-date on the Cambridge professor."

The next morning a package was delivered to my room with Nicola curious what was in the large envelope. When she found out we were to have a flat in London to live on occasion, she was excited. Nicola couldn't wait to discuss where the flat should be with David's girlfriend.

While we were checking out Kenny walked into the foyer to take the Thibodeau's to London Heathrow for their flight to Washington. The four of us went to London to start looking for a nice place to rent.

The girls looked at places while I went with David to the bench where some of clandestine meetings were held between the ambassador and the Russians. David stayed at the bench while I walked back to find the best building to set up our ops center. Nicola wanted to find one south facing without knowing why we had to be in this area.

After several hours we found the right furnished townhouse that had two bedrooms and a fantastic view over Hyde Park, and the benches around the lake. The one we picked cost more per week than Nicola made as a school teacher. We put down a deposit and told the estate agent we would be back this coming Thursday to take possession and pick up the keys. The locks had to be changed without the owners or the estate agent knowing why. The budget was open ended with Simpson okaying the operations controlled from Thibodeau's Washington office, so not to alert the ambassador.

It was set; the four of us would christen the new flat with a bottle of champagne this Friday night. Nicola and I went to Harrow, while David and his girlfriend went back to Cambridge.

Monday morning I was back in the flat in Cambridge with Leos and Monika already gone. Since my first class was canceled, I went to see Professor North in the hospital. He was glad to see me with a little feeling of ambiguity, which was not like him to be unsure about anything. This may be a good sign that he was ready to become a changed man. I really couldn't freely talk to him in this ward. His accommodation had to be changed before he was let out to go home and be demeaned by his wife.

We discussed his feelings about being here in the ward. He did not like going to the toilet in the middle of the huge split ward with his gown having to be held together with his hands. After being asked if he would like a private room, he told me his wife would not pay for such extravagance.

However, he conveyed if it was her he would gladly pay. I told him to let me see what I can do, and then planted the seed of indifference to her by asking him as I was leaving why is she so bitter or unhappy all of the time.

Downstairs in the admitting office I asked a female clerk how much it would cost for a friend who has a national health card to pay for a private room for a week since he has become agoraphobic. I was told the price was five pounds a day and wrote a check out of the new business account. An orderly was called to have Professor North moved to his room. I went back to prepare him and hopefully be moved before his wife showed up. Luck was not with me as I heard his wife's sharp voice calling out "Hey you!" I turned around just before going in to the ward.

She said, "You owe me an explanation for not showing up yesterday, you idiot, you probably forgot. I want some answers right now."

"I am dreadfully sorry, I was called away to visit a friend from Germany in London who had to leave right away to go back."

"You will answer my questions now."

"Not here Jane with so many people around."

"Alright, come with me, we can talk at my home, where no one can hear you explain who you actually are."

She led me by my arm out of the hospital and into a taxi. At her house she put on the kettle for a cup of tea and told me to sit down at the kitchen table. It was an understatement to say I had to think fast about what to say. I excused myself to go to the loo to buy some more time. With standing by the sink and seeing the window I climbed into earlier, I thought of something the professor said. In a roundabout way Jane was tight with money as her husband languished in a hospital ward.

Back in the kitchen now, she loudly said, "Well, let's have it!"

With sipping my tea to help form a convincing story she was getting agitated.

I said, "A friend of mine I grew up with from the German Democratic Republic, who is a member of the Stasi network, told me of a plot to kill you and your husband."

"Why would they want to kill me? I have nothing to do with my husband's work."

"Unfortunately Jane, there were multiple KGB agents killed visiting you and your husband in the last two years. Your association with the American Ambassador confirmed you both are working both sides of the street. That is why your home was broken into to get the paperwork your husband has on the American connection."

"I never met the American any of the times my husband went to London. His notes are kept pinned under his mattress and nowhere close to his desk. Who do you work for and why did you help us escape or were you paid to help us, if so by whom?"

"Who met you at Heathrow when you arrived?"

"He said he was a home office employee."

"Do you have his card, no probably not? He was a MI5 agent. Ask yourself this question: Who notified the home office? What ID did I show the British

Airline pilot? Now this is what you should know; I work for two completely different countries," I said with a serious look on my face.

"Jane, we would like to offer you a business proposal. We are willing to offer you two payments of 500 pounds each at six-month intervals for your husband's help in recruiting young, bright students, who are conservative in their outlook. He has to drop his communist manifesto."

"These students will be future employees of the home office or become civil servants. The main reason you should come over to our side is you and your husband are being pursued by the Russians. We will provide security and safety for you and the professor. If you decline, this meeting never took place. Are you able to coerce your husband to help us?"

"Of course I can, when do I receive my first payment?"

"Now."

"Let me have it then, I will call your bluff, you are all talk."

"You do understand that you are working for us now; we do require your loyalty."

"I do promise to be loyal if it is worthwhile and obey you only, no one else."

The check couldn't be filled out fast enough as Jane reached for the fortune before the ink was dry. With the check coming out of the firm's account, it was no concern of mine as I wasn't footing the unsavory debt. This was a good time to let Mrs. North know that her husband was now in a private hospital room where she can start to work on him. I also asked for his notes that were squirreled away under his mattress. She went up to get the notes after she had the check in her hand. Someone once said that money was a control agent; they were right on with Mrs. North. After being handed the damaging notes, I left to speak to the professor.

Back at Addenbrooke's, Rodney was in his room and as I put a bunch of tulips from Amsterdam in his urinal vase; he laughed and said, "I will not be needing thing anymore. Thank you for getting my wife and me out of that dreadful situation in Berlin. Thank you for also rescuing me from that dreadful ward. Please help me fill in the missing pieces as you are the only one who can. What happened after that brute knocked me out. I was still concussed without being seen to by a physician when they threw me into a freezing damp cell."

"After dodging a punch you threw towards my nose, I stumbled backwards, and saw the Russian throw a punch as he reached for a gun at the same time. You were knocked out before falling backwards and you kicked the hand with the revolver in it, making it go off and killing him from what I could see."

"So I did kill him. They will not settle until they have me back in a Soviet prison, too many of their agents have been killed who are or were associated with me. Is there anything that could be done to protect my wife and myself? I don't know why I am asking you except I have a feeling you really can help us."

"Your wife has been briefed on your security and will tell you everything. I have to go and let you get some rest before Mrs. North visits you."

I was expected at the vicar's to have tea with the vicar this morning. The vicar's wife served us tea in the mansion's lounge. There were a few boxing trophy's on the mantel piece.

I asked him, "Were you a boxer? It doesn't go with being a priest."

"You are right as the sport is different today than it was when gentlemen played the sport. When one wins one should have the compassion for the loser, not berate him. It doesn't seem to be that way for our American cousins. I thought Henry Cooper was a truly good sport by the way he handled himself when the title was taken away from him by shameless trickery. It is hard to get that ripped glove out from one's mind. We must continue on though."

Our conversation soon was on the North's as the vicar was amazed the professor had time to talk to him; in the past, he would have been ignored even while performing university duties. Mrs. North is still a little prickly according to him and after the service she walked out as the final blessing was started. He was happy that she did sit through a sermon aimed at her in a manner that would cause her to ponder during the week.

Early Thursday afternoon David and I went to London to set up the flat into an operational surveillance base and as a safe house. David was asked to go the bench that was used by the KGB and plant a listening device. Benches on the sides, if used, were tested to see if the tiny device could pick up conversation. The receiver did pick up the sounds from David as long as he did not whisper. That would have to do for the time being.

With him sitting on the middle bench and switching to the other two, I found the best window to observe from a top window in what they call a box room. A box room is one that is too small for a bedroom. I whistled for him to come in from the cold weather and we would set up the surveillance point. We both had various suggestions on how the room should be arranged. The main piece of furniture had to be an elevated seat with a place to write, hold binoculars, a coffee cup and the radio on a flat surface.

The next job was to paint the room flat black along with the back of the door, and to take out all of the light bulbs. Now there was the task of finding a good pub to take our girlfriends tomorrow night. After trying several places, we found one with an old Victorian feel with large leather chairs and benches. It was across the street from the flat.

The next morning Kenny picked us up to have breakfast at a cafe across from the Russian safe house. While we were sitting in a booth where

David could see the front door a thought came to me. Kenny was sure a KGB replacement was not here as of this morning. I inquired where I could purchase a uniform that electricity engineers wear so to disguise myself and plant a bug in the telephone. There was such a place outside Victoria Station.

The three of us worked all morning setting up the Russian flat and having lunch at a pub overlooking the American Embassy.

David was told that he would be living in the flat over the Easter holidays and the long school break while I was out of the country. They were curious to where I would be and why for that long. They thought it was a bit much that I would be in sunny Florida while they worked in a cold climate.

However, when I told them I would be in a Soviet Bloc country for two weeks, they decided that being here wasn't so bad after all. The American ambassador walked in the door as we were about to get up. David was told to wait a minute, and was made to study the man while I got up to pay.

Kenny dropped us back at the flat and had a good look around at our ops center. I set up a separate phone to ring when the one at the Russian flat was used. We were in business. Kenny was impressed as he walked into the dark room and looked out the window to see why we were in this particular flat.

Over the next few weeks we learned the name of the new KGB agent posted to London, he is Igor Antipov. It is unbelievable that the same Russian safe house was being used after being broke into several times, losing documents and lots of cash. They really can't be that aloof on their security. If it was me, I would now find another safe house and use this one as a trap in which to bait. Kenny did say he would keep an eye out to see if another address was being used by the foreigner, and would ask his mates if they motored the man to another address.

I said to Kenny and David, "If I were the foreign agent, I would make sure of using as many different taxis as possible, even if it meant walking a block or two for the reason of not setting up a routine. Kenny, when you ask your mates, ask how many taxis he has used to the same address if he is playing sneaky. I was also wondering why a replacement wasn't in place by now."

"Right you are, Guv."

Kenny was just leaving as the girls walked in. They were glad to see him again so soon. The weekend went fast and we all left Monday morning very early to get to our respective homes. Back in Cambridge, I went to see the professor. He must be feeling a lot better. I went to his house and Jane was glad to see me as she acted nice for a change.

I asked Rodney, "What has got into your wife? She seems happy."

He laughed and said, "I really have no idea, Ludwig, she acts like she did when we were young and not married, so independent. It is nice to have the young girl attitude back in her. Now she told me you work for two different countries or the way you put it to her, two firms at the same time. I want my papers back as soon as possible. Did you read them, I hope not because they are private."

"No, I did not read them and the answer to your other question is you have to contact MI5 if you want the notes back. I was paid to deliver you. I would have thought you might have learned something with your experiences in a country with a Marxist agenda. Do you think citizens in Great Britain should be treated as you were when they are suspected of an offense? You are not safe on this planet as the Soviets want you brought back to face charges."

My attitude was: *I've had it with that guy who runs with the hounds and runs with the fox.* Mrs. North showed me to the door and stepped outside to tell me not to worry about her husband. I told her about the new KGB agent called Igor, and if he called to let me know when he wants to meet up with her husband. So far she is turning out to be an asset.

I had to spend more time living in London while David and Leos kept tabs on the Norths. David would call every time the Apostles met. Mrs. North called to say that her husband was meeting the Russian agent in London tomorrow, which is Saturday. She had no idea what time. It was very strange that the Russian phone never made a ring as to who had arranged the meeting. There must be another safe house the KGB was using. I called David to come to London tonight. I needed him tomorrow morning. He wanted to bring his girlfriend and had to be dissuaded to do so with work to be done. Nicola called after she got out of school and wanting to see me tonight.

I had to tell her that David and I had to work this weekend, and it would be inconvenient; how about next weekend? She agreed.

David walked past our local pub and saw me inside. He came in and ordered a beer. After we finished our drink, we walked to the flat to discuss tomorrow's schedule.

Now in the flat I told him about the meeting with the professor and the Russian. I wanted to have pictures taken from the other side of the lake when they met. He must not see us taking photographs as our operation would be compromised.

"The usual setup with the Russian is he will wait in some obscure place until the professor walks by on the way to the meeting point. He would follow about 100 yards behind. If he didn't follow him, that means there is another person attending the same meeting. The Russian will then follow the middle man and this is how it will go down," I explained.

"I will be the one taking the photographs and you turn the tapes on as soon as there are together. When they break up, and if there is a third man, you will follow him. Do not let him see you and if you lose sight of him that means he is suspicious of being followed and has ducked into a shop to see who walks by. Keep walking towards the closest tube station and wait inside until he gets there. Board the tube in the furthermost compartment toward the rear. Follow him to where he gets off and wait for him to clear the ramp. If he stays on the platform waiting for the train to take off, go to the next station and get off and walk back towards the station he got off. Chances are he will live between the two stops. Be careful because he has already seen you up close from a shop window.

"Leave me to follow the Russian and letting the professor go because we know where he will be tomorrow. We will meet at Flanagan's. Go downstairs to the dining room so we would be able to see if you were being followed as that was the only way in to the restaurant.

"Now let's go get an outfit that an angler would wear while fishing, from the closest sports out fitters. I will need an oil skin parka, rainproof floppy hat and a fishing pole with a creel to hide the camera in."

The next morning after breakfast we waited what seemed hours. Waiting is the most difficult as one has to deal with the boredom of surveillance.

At 11 a.m. I took off to make a hide on the other side of the lake. After making a grass and reed hide, I waited another two hours getting colder by the minute. I thought next time David is going to be the one waiting in the weeds and I will be in the cozy flat drinking cups of tea.

It was after 2 p.m. when a man sat on the bench; he looked familiar even from 200 yards. It had to be the ambassador. No one else was around, probably because snow was forecast and it was now sleeting. Not long after the ambassador arrived, the professor showed up and a couple of minutes later the KGB agent walked up. I took photographs of them being introduced and shaking hands. After taking almost a roll of film, I left to get out of the wet clothes and have a cup of tea.

By the time I changed with strapping a confiscated Russian Luger and holster on under my jacket, and drinking the tea, the meeting broke up. David and I hurried down to the street to follow our targets. The professor and the Russian headed off together. The ambassador was David's responsibility. I had it a little easier as the professor was having a conversation with the KGB agent as they walked towards Hyde Park Corner tube station, with the ambassador and David walking left towards the embassy. It was ironic that we came within a few feet of each other while stalking our prey.

I followed my two targets into the nearest station where we all boarded a train that was terminating at Hammersmith. A discarded newspaper was convenient to use as a way to hide behind. The two agents got off at the last stop and walked towards the river Thames, still highly engaged in conversation. They walked down a few steps and got on an old painted house boat, most likely the Russians new safe house.

The professor stayed for hours, and as the light was fading the Russian looked out of a window before closing the tiny curtain and putting a light on.

I could now edge closer to hear their conversation. The sidewalk by the river led alongside the long boat. The river flowing toward the back of the barge meant my footsteps could not be heard with the wind direction helping.

I was still watching and listening when Big Ben struck 10. Leaning against the river wall was only interrupted when someone had a pee in the river on the opposite side of the boat. About 45 minutes later a heated argument broke out with the Russian evidently drunk on vodka. He was speaking Russian in a loud, menacing manner and the professor loudly squeaking something in retaliation.

The next thing I knew was the two of them was on the back deck shoving each other with the professor being pushed into the Thames. I still needed the self-aggrandizing jerk in Cambridge to finish a job. I hurried onto the front of the barge and through the interior towards the back end. The Russian was shouting, "Serves you right, you are going to die tonight in your precious river."

It was an easy maneuver to thump the big Russian between the shoulder blades with him leaning towards the water. Using the palms of both hands it was effortless to propel him into the river. I looked for something to drag the professor back to the barge and found a long pole with a grappling hook on the end to pull the now almost drowned professor close enough to grab his sweater and pull him on board. The Russian went down for the third time and floated away with the tide.

I put the jerk on his stomach to force the water out. He started spewing up river water and vodka, and I left him then to go inside and rummage through the Russian's personal effects. His briefcase was tucked inside his clothes closet and was taken out and set down by the front exit. A phone box was a few yards down on the opposite side of the street. I called Kenny to come get me and drive the professor back to Cambridge. He knew exactly where we were as he had taken the ambassador there a few days ago.

When Kenny drove up I threw a couple of blankets onto the floor of his taxi to lay the professor on in case the jerk still had river water in his stomach. As I was getting the Russian's gear, an old lady called out the window to ask what we were doing. I whispered to Kenny to tell her we caught a monster of a fish. She threatened to call the police if we made any more noise. Kenny asked her in his Cockney brogue that she should call the old bill.

Kenny dropped me off at my London flat and continued on to Cambridge and to take the professor to Addenbrooke's Hospital. I asked him to come by in the morning to go over our story in case someone reported his taxi being in the vicinity of a crime.

David got out of bed when he heard me open the door, and commented that I smell like an old dead fish.

I said, "I put the old fish in Kenny's cab. The Russian is dead, drowned in the Thames and the professor was fished out of the river before he drowned. How was your day?"

"The Yank went straight to his flat next to the embassy and I was back here within an hour."

"What about the conversation among the three men by the park bench, anything to report?"

"The ambassador is a definitely a double agent, you have got him by the short and curlies. Everything you suspected will be backed up on the tapes."

"Good, I will call General Simpson right now and have him over here in the morning."

The general was not thrilled to be wakened at 2 a.m. He will be here at 8 a.m. sharp for coffee.

The next morning we struggled to be ready for the general, but managed to get the coffee percolator on. Last night was a long ordeal, not as long as Kenny's with driving to Cambridge and back to London. There was a knock on the door, probably the general. David went downstairs to let him into the building. It was Kenny just getting back to report that the sick professor was in the hospital, and wanted me to tell him what happened as he stayed flat down on the taxi's floor all the way to Cambridge. The men and women in the white coats said he would be in the same room as before. Someone will have to come by and pay for the extra days. He had a credit of two days and then an account would have to be set up.

The general walked in as I left the bottom door ajar for him; he was handed a mug of strong black coffee. After making a fresh pot of coffee I joined everyone at the table by the window.

General Simpson said as he took a sip, "Ug this is strong, and if it doesn't get this old heart started nothing will. You men look terrible, have you been on the booze all night?"

Kenny replied, "No mate, been driving one of your assets as you like to call im to the orsepital. See you later, Guv."

"Okay Kenny, kick the wedge out of the door downstairs so it will close. See you later next weekend, maybe at Flanagan's. I owe you a meal out."

When we heard the door close, our briefing started with explanations from the start of the surveillance to when Kenny came in this morning. I poured everyone another cup of coffee and David started the tapes. The ambassador was definitely a traitor, or at least working both sides of the pond.

The most damaging piece of information was that he would go through CIA dispatches to obtain names of who was involved in European operations, especially concerning the recent extractions in Berlin, Prague and Leipzig.

The general was aghast at what was on the tapes; however, he needed photographs to close the lid on the scoundrel. He couldn't believe the good job that was done, especially when he was given the roll of film.

General Simpson said, "You two men are wonderful. If the film comes out we can close down this operation next week and hand back the keys."

"Sorry sir, I had to sign a year's lease to get this particular apartment."

"Looks like you boys have a great get away place now. Tell me Wright, what are you going to do with the professor? He doesn't seem to be very bright. You would think being saved from being killed he would owe you something. He seems to go back to the other side as soon as he is able to walk again."

"I know General. He has used up his nine lives before this weekend and now he does have a service to do. I can send you a report monthly as soon as you get another ambassador in place that is trustworthy."

"Nixon will appoint a much better ambassador, I can assure you. The last two presidents were complete reprobates. Can you imagine appointing a commie-loving booze runner to serve in the Court of St. James? What a travesty that posting was. Now let's see what is in the KGB agent's briefcase. First, we have to see if it is booby trapped."

The briefcase wasn't tainted as the general pried it open with a screwdriver. There were more damning transmissions between Moscow and the American Embassy. There was a large amount of cash, two passports and a gun. The general gave me the gun with ammunition; he winked as he told me I knew what to do with it. The cash was to be mingled with any other left- over funds for future operations. He then left and would see us next weekend here at the flat.

After the general was gone I went to Harrow to spend the rest of the day and night with Nicola. I wanted to take her and her parents out to the pub for a drink, and then to dinner at their favorite restaurant. David and I planned to meet tomorrow afternoon in the Cambridge flat.

The next morning I was at Addenbrooke's before 8 a.m. and watching Rodney sleeping. After disabling his call and pulling up a chair in his private room I whispered in his ears, "Wakey, wakey!" It startled him as he woke up to see me six inches from his face. He somehow knew this was not a visit to discuss my grades. He reached for the call cord that wasn't there. He started to get up and out of bed. He now was starting to be irritating, and needed some counseling and calmly telling him that he was not useful anymore.

"What are you going to do now Rodney? The Russians almost murdered you again. That was your last chance to stay alive. You are considered to be a lost cause now by the two firms who ordered me to keep you safe."

"Please Ludwig, I won't stray again, I promise. Just tell me what you want me to do and I will do it."

"From this day forward you will not spew your venomous hatred for the Americans or their allies. You are not allowed to meet any foreign people here in Britain or travel to another country for a meeting. If you go against these commands, the firm will give away damaging information to Scotland Yard. You will be implicated in the murder of Volkov,

Malenkov, and now Antipov. I do not want to see you again, and if I do it will be the last person you see before getting to the underworld. Do we have a working agreement? Oh yes, you will fix it that I have attended classes everyday and passed with honors."

"Who are you really? How did you know I was on that long boat? I would like some answers, please."

"Piss off!"

I got up and placed the chair back against the wall, fixed his call cord to where he could reach it, and left the room. I waited to bump into Mrs. North downstairs.

She looked frightened when she saw me, I told her. "Sorry Jane, your husband broke the agreement we had. You are no longer needed."

Jane watched me leave through the entrance as I had to hurry to their house to finish up our association once and for all. At the rear of the residence it was simple to enter through the French doors that were wedged closed the last time I was in the house. It took a short time to find the rest of the money she hid from cashing the firm's check and then leaving the house to see Leos and Monika before moving to London.

Leos understood I had to start another chapter in my CIA life. Monika was emotional and thanked me for everything. They were told to stay in the flat until the end of the school year, and to keep an eye on Rodney. Kenny was picking me up at 1 p.m. after I meet with David over lunch.

When David showed up and seen the suit cases he asked, "Who's leaving?"

"I am David; this operation is over thanks to you and the others. Call me when you want to meet up in London. Keep an eye on Rodney, I think he will be okay from now on; we had a heart-to-heart talk and he did see the errors of his ways. Kenny is here, see you David."

# Chapter 7

## Briefing on Boca Grande

Christmas week was magical with Nicola and me attending so many parties with her relatives and friends. We painted the black room back to a white room in the Hyde Park flat, where we spent many nights enjoying this vibrant city. We flew to Gasparilla Island the day after Christmas, staying close to the Boca Grande Village. The three generals and their wives joined us later that week.

Saturday afternoon I had a briefing with the generals as the wives and Nicola walked to the village. We thought about staying on the sister island, Little Gasparilla Island; but with no bridges, it would have been hard for the older ladies to get on and off boats.

The briefing was held on an abandoned phosphate dock at the south end of the island, with us sitting on a rail overlooking the Boca Grande Pass with its waters infested with giant hammerheads and vicious bull sharks. The three generals were surprised on the remoteness of this virtually unknown part of Florida. Our meeting was headed by General

Thibodeau as he explain why the reason for such secrecy.

Thibodeau started with the assignment goals as he said, "Wright, the three of us have gone over a scenario involving an agent stirring up the populace movement in the Czech Republic. The CIA is monitoring a group of students from influential leaders and one Czech army general. General Senja is a name you should remember as he is contemplating a defection to the West. We would like an agent to go in and provide help with money and logistics. We need the Russian's to overreact and show the world how they can quell a protest. You will get involved by staying in the background and not become a front-line protester. If you are arrested, there is a good chance you will be interrogated, and not having any background it could be fatal."

"Yes sir, I will need to act out a new background if I go over as a West German or as an English exchange student. Thinking about it now a foreign student may be the best cover, perhaps from the United Kingdom since English is my language. For the funding, how much am I allowed?"

General Neuhofer said, "We have pondered that question many times and came up with the sum of $30,000, which should be about 450,000 Czech crowns."

"You will have to be in Bad Aibling one day after you get back to London. Your team is preparing themselves for your place of crossing by camping out in the Bohemia Forest as we speak. Your expected time of being in Czechoslovakia is four months or until the end of the Easter break is over with. Are there any other things you need?"

"Yes sir, I would like someone to train me in a day or two on how to subconsciously act out a falsehood if I were to be interrogated. Rumor has it, there was such a person in England during the Second World War.

General Simpson added, "There is an English psychotherapist who had worked with a group of British spies that was successful in infiltrating different regiments of the Germany's Third Reich, including the Gestapo. He may be available since he has retired, and living on a British pension doesn't exactly provide extra spending money.

General Thibodeau broke up the briefing as he had a guide waiting to take him and the other generals fishing. By the time I walked to the beach house, Nicola was back from shopping as the three wives had to start packing for leaving early the next morning.

Unfortunately, we had to leave Boca Grande a few days earlier than expected as I had to meet a psychotherapist in London in his time frame.

Since the shrink was busy after all, he made time for two days of his choosing. I had to be there or wait another four weeks to be analyzed and trained in something he called mind developmental.

Nicola and I arrived in Heathrow on the red eye without sleeping as we talked all the way across the Atlantic. Kenny dropped her off first in Harrow on the way to my place in London. It was almost noon as I finished unpacking and the door bell rang. It was the shrink General Simpson hired to transform me into a British subject. He was an overweight older gentleman in a dirty gray coat from the 1930s. He was slightly stooped with a mustache, which looked like it was used to strain his beer before it entered his mouth. His demeanor matched his name as he introduced himself as Bartholomew.

I politely asked, "Sir, I have had little sleep in the past 36 hours and would like for you to come back in the morning."

"Nonsense, you Yanks need toughening up. Now let's get started after I hook up the machinery."

I must have dozed off as he fumbled around for a long time setting up his camera and recording equipment. The next thing I knew I was laying on the floor with my chair on its side. He must have kicked the chair out from under me as I slept.

He sat me in the same chair and hypnotized me in seconds. The old goat woke me up to watch my reactions on the movie projector.

I was astounded he had something that recorded that fast and had me under hypnoses within a few seconds. The time I was out was over half an hour with me doing all types of physical training exercises.

He said, "You are going to be easy to train as it took no time at all for me to have you under my control. This the easy part, think of someone you know in the British Isles you could impersonate; it would be nice if he was dead so a trail could not be found leading to your real identity."

"My grandfather has passed away years ago; he was of Scottish and Irish ancestry. He immigrated to America at the turn of the century; his name was

Malcolm McLeod and was a bit of a rogue from what I have been told."

"Good, now let's get back to work and have you become him in your subconscious as you need to emulate a Scotsman."

I don't remember him putting me back under again; and as he snapped me out of it, he had me make a cup of tea while he got the projector back to where we could watch me being another person. I was astounded watching me answering questions in an English accent that sounded like his.

He said, "Now for another game, think of a story that will get you out of trouble if you are arrested. You will have to come up with something a captor wants or a value that would benefit one of your torturers. I will be back at 8 a.m., and try not to have too many beers tonight."

As soon as he was gone I called General Simpson to have a passport made with my new identity and an address in Glasgow in the rough area called the Gorbals. The new passport would be delivered tomorrow afternoon along with the $30,000 in $100 notes. Next was Nicola, who would like to know how the transformation was progressing. After hanging up the phone I went to the pub for a beer and supper before going to bed. It has been two days without sleep, except when the shrink put me asleep.

The story conjured up during the night that would be beneficial to anyone who was lucky enough to capture me without being killed, and finding out where the agency's money was hidden.

At precisely 8 a.m. the door bell rang with the psychiatrist wanting in to start the continuation of my transcendental subconscious story. A cup of tea was offered as he wanted to think about my story before incorporating it into my physic.

He wasted no time as he asked, "Have you been pondering an escape scenario?"

"Yes sir, I have. First thing for me to do when I cross into the unknown is to bury one-third of my cash along with a handgun to be unearthed later if someone is guarding me. Then farther down the path, I would bury a smaller amount in a shallow grave as a teaser in case it was needed to lure a captor into a trap. On top of both graves a decomposing animal may have to be placed to ward off the person or persons wanting to dig up the stash themselves and have me do the dirty job."

"Very good Malcolm McLeod; it may save your life one day. Now let's get started, I promise by the end of the next eight hours you will be Malcolm McLeod in your subconscious, even with being pushed to the limits."

Bartholomew started his machines running just before he hypnotized me. When I was under, two men were let in as I saw later in the projection. They first took all of my clothes off, and then threw me in the bath face down.

Almost being killed with so much water ingested in the stomach and lungs, it took them an hour to get me back on my feet after pushing water out of my body. Unbelievable as I watched on film being beaten by rubber hoses, leaving welts on my buttocks and shoulders. The deeper the hurt administered the more I became Malcolm McLeod. It's unbelievable how the mind takes over in such extreme punishment. Welts were appearing in the slow-motion grainy film.

The most bizarre thing to watch was the hypnotist convincing me I had been without sleep for a week. My speech was slurred as I sounded inebriated trying to string distinguishable words together to get a point across. They knew they broke me when

I started crying and asking for my mother, all of this in a British accent. I was asked my mother's name and thankfully it was so English. The three of them on film showed their satisfaction as they shook hands.

The transformation took several hours longer than what was expected and after 7 p.m. the two masochists left.

My nude body was not the most shocking part of this sleepy ordeal. When I was snapped out of the trance my hair was wet and my body smelling like someone threw up on it. The movie was over with me crying and telling the torturers to please let me sleep as I told them where the money was buried in the forest.

Bartholomew asked, "Are you satisfied or should we do it all over again? I think you came through this with full marks. I must say Yank, you did not break easily. I will be off now, good luck on your next assignment."

When he was downstairs he called up to say a courier was looking for me. I signed for the package and went back upstairs to bath and sleep.

I woke up the next morning so sore it took time to run a hot bath to soak my body, without making a cup of coffee. My mind was still trying to figure out what was really on the movie, and how scary it was to see me being broken.

Finally, the brain was working as I kept adding hot water as I figured out that I'd slept for 12 uninterrupted hours. Remembering that a delivery was made, I climbed out of the bath to make a cup of coffee and find the documents needed for the next assignment. I opened the package to see the money in a belt designed to hold American currency, along with airline tickets to Frankfurt and one fake passport with the name of Malcolm McLeod.

Instructions were inside a folder with a wax seal. I had to meet General Neuhofer at Frankfurt Airport, and be briefed as I was driven to Frankfurt's ASA headquarters to pick up my car. Then drive to Hof where the team would be waiting for my arrival in the quartermaster's warehouse.

Getting to Frankfurt the next morning, the general was waiting outside on the curb as his driver met me coming through customs.

Once in the green sedan, I asked Neuhofer, "Why Hof? First, I have to go to the Bad Aibling Base to pick up my gear and a uniform."

"Your gear is packed and on the bus waiting for you."

"Sir, what about..."

He interrupted me and said, "Yes, everything, your revolvers with holsters and silencers. I don't want to know why you would need those and I never have been informed of you possessing firearms."

I was dropped off without anymore instructions. He did say we are to be back at the same Florida location where I was to be debriefed sometime in April.

The long trip gave me time to think about how to handle the crossing. It was going to save time as the team had observed the border area for the past week. As I pulled into the Hof Base, the team was out as I drove behind the quartermaster's building. We were all glad to see each other and Summerall scheduled our briefing over in the mess hall as we ate an early supper.

In the briefing, a report of border activity for the past week showed more troop movements than normal. They thought that was because of most of our past crossings happened between Christmas and New Year's Day.

On the bus were the motorbike and the Russian Colonel's uniform. As we drove to the bivouac area, I got dressed and then had another briefing on how this was going to be handled if certain problems arose.

Summerall asked, "When do you want to cross? It won't be dark for another hour."

"Sir, I would like to go as soon as possible. There are a few jobs I have to do before arriving in Plzen and Prague."

The first sergeant asked, "Would one of your jobs have anything to do with the pretty daughter of the hotel owner?"

"No first sergeant, that isn't one of my first priorities. I have to dig two graves on the way to the main road before it gets to dark."

Everyone found the first sergeant's question and my reply comical. There was someone missing from the team. Buck was at the crossing area watching for any bad guys, or guys with weapons.

When we got to the border, the first sergeant gave me a small Army shovel in which to dig the graves. We tied the shovel onto the bike and walked towards the border. Buck was glad to see me and couldn't believe I was crossing this evening without thinking it over.

I told them all, "Remember in the past, if you hear gunshots do not come over or I may shoot you by mistake. Again, as before, if there is trouble and I am okay I will fire three rounds five seconds apart. If not, be back here the first weekend in April or on Good Friday. How many rounds of ammo do I have and did you guys make sure all the chambers are full?"

Summerall said, "All chambers are full and you have 20 extra rounds; now go before it is to dark to start your digging, and good luck Wright."

After crossing and finding the familiar foxhole we had used before, I dug a small hole to plant one gun and $5,000. A half- eaten deer was close-by, and I dragged its carcass across the area to ward off soldiers; it was pretty smelly.

Near the road I dug another hole to bury $1,000. I shot a rabbit with the silencer on the barrel of the gun and opened the hare up to scoop out its insides with the shovel and place the money inside its carcass. After placing a large limb over the buried money and rabbit, and another large limb on top of that one to make sure no critter could get to the carcass and disrupt the money trap, I pushed the bike towards the main road.

After stopping on the edge of the forest and pulling the infrared binoculars from around my neck to survey the immediate area for warm human bodies was important. There were no signs of anything but deer in the forest or any vehicle noise on the highway.

The motorbike cranked up on the first attempt as it got me on the way to the first stop at Hotel Areal in Horni Bezdekov where I hoped to spend a few days. I pulled up in front of the hotel with Lenka running out the door to welcome me back.

"Ludwig, what is that smell? Did you drive over something on the road on the way here, it's terrible," Lenka said.

"Yes, my darling, I need to have these leathers and clothes washed along with myself before we have breakfast. Where are your parents? Can I park the bike in the garage before having a bath?"

"Yes, you can park in the barn. My mother and papa are on their annual ski holiday in Yugoslavia for three weeks. They left one day ago, isn't that wonderful. How long will you stay this time?"

"At least two days and maybe up to a week. I will have to go to Prague on Saturday to see a friend and will be back in the evening if that is okay."

"Yes, yes, it is good, stay as long as you like. Your room is paid for anyway until the end of the month. We feel terrible that you pay for a year in advance and stay maybe one week in total."

After parking the bike Lenka had a bath drawn with a cup of tea resting on the edge of the tub. I forgot about the belt marks on my back, which was a shock to Lenka seeing them for the first time. The hot water was as relaxing and welcoming as ever. There were still bruises from last week's torture, and this soaking bath was helping in making them go away or at least they felt like the bruising was fading. As I got out of the bath Lenka came back upstairs with some type of ointment to help the swelling go away. She didn't believe me when I told her the beating was from a training course requiring military personal to go through.

While having our meal I asked Lenka, "There is a rumor the students are planning a revolt from the new government forcing out the popular president. How do you feel about the protesters in your country?"

"I also am upset with the foreign rulers putting in a puppet to help the Russian's keep all of my people prisoners in their own country. We had more freedoms as you know last year, and now there are more authorities stopping us and asking questions. There are a group of students from wealthy families near Plzen attending Charles University that stop here to stay before meeting other friends in Plzen. I overhear them say crazy things like when the tanks come in, they will lie on the road to stop them. They know I am okay with their cause and talk freely in front of me as I serve them food and drinks. Ludwig, you are not thinking about getting mixed up with the movement are you? Please do not join them."

"Lenka, I have to help and need you to listen to me. If I do get involved and am arrested, can you go to my room and read a note asking you to do me a favor. I will not be physically involved, but hope to help in the way of providing money and coordinate the planning. The chances of me getting arrested are very remote. The less you know the better off you will be, so please, no questions from now on."

We both look forward to the walks in the forest with her dog Sasha tramping through the light covering of snow for hours for a couple of days.

Saturday was suddenly here and I had to go see the Gypsy leader and friend at the Prague Flea Market to exchange some dollars.

Leaving early I was at the market as they opened its gates, and was one of the first to walk through. My Gypsy friend was setting up his marquee when he saw me walk in. He stopped what he was doing and gave me a big hug. His clan members being curious and also glad to see me again gathered outside his marquee to see what we were going to do. He told them all to go about their business. After exchanging $5,000 into Czech Korunas or Crowns, someone called with a promise he would be able to exchange the rest of the dollars next Saturday.

I spent the morning with him and had lunch served to us by his beautiful daughter. She was still at the university and I took the opportunity to ask her about the unrest in the community. She was worried that students will be quashed by the military with their large trucks and tanks. Her father Topol was astounded hearing that the students were planning an uprising. He wanted to know if I could stop the uprising with his daughter telling him no one can stop this now, it is too late.

Topol asked, "Is that why you are here, English?"

"Yes that is the reason. Your daughter is right; no one can stop the people from protesting. A lot of the protesters will be killed. The world will be watching to see how the Russians handle the situation. Do you have relatives or clan members in Plzen that you could introduce me to? I may need their help if things go bad."

"I will take you Monday morning. Where will I meet you?"

"I will be at the traffic circle near the Areal Botanika on the way to Cheb at 8 a.m., or do you want to make it later that morning?"

"Yes, English that will be good, 8 a.m. Now you must go before the police show up this afternoon. My wife has family in the Plzen Gypsy village; they are part of my clan. My daughter does not have a suitor and wanted me to ask you if you have married your girlfriend."

The daughter, being embarrassed by her dad, got up to go to the wagon with me following her. I caught up with her at the back deck area and gave her a hug as she returned the gesture and gave me a long, full kiss on the lips. She was really happy now and insinuated that if it wasn't for her papa, we would have never taken this first step. She was as beautiful as she was intelligent, and this was a spark that started a fire in both of us that wasn't going to be easy to extinguish.

As I was leaving, her father headed me off to give me a hug and welcomed me to the family. I cannot think there will be a happy ending to this episode, especially with Topol wanting to protect his daughter and me not wanting to be in this kind of predicament. I may end up losing a friend and a good ally for future covert actions.

While leaving the big Gypsy said, "You are like a son I never had; it is good that you may be family soon."

He laughed as he was motioning me to go, I wasn't sure if he was being serious or teasing. It was worrying if he really thought I could actual fit in his clan.

# Chapter 8

## Prague's Second Spring Uprising Attempt

Back at Lenka's, there were several bicycles leaning against the front of the hotel. When I walked in, the group stared at me as Lenka came over and told them it was okay as she has known me for a long time. Lenka then introduced me as her good friend from West Germany, and a fellow student of theirs. Studying them I found they were all self-assured young men, except for one who had wandering eyes with an uncomfortable or uneasy demeanor. I decided that one character was not to be trusted or at least for now be kept at arm's length; he was the only one that gave off bad vibes with being quiet and aloof.

The leader of the group was introduced as Antonin, an outspoken individual who was okay with speaking English since his German was inadequate. We all had dinner together and socialized afterwards. The shifty one tried his best to expose me as an impostor, and the more alcohol he consumed the more belligerent he became. He finally got to the point of my ethnicity and accused me of being a Brit or even worse an American over here stirring up the people. By now he was out of his head with the group's leader wanting him to be taken to his room.

Shifty was my name for him; he was not going to go to his room and became more defiant and aggressive. All of his friends seemed to be against him tonight, which made him show his true colors as a mixed up young man. The tipping point was when he told everyone the Russians will kill all of the dissidents and he will be glad to fire the first shot. Antonin ordered him to get out and leave the group forever.

With the awkwardness subsiding and the obstinate offender on his way back to Prague, most of the group went to bed. Antonin and I were left alone with having one more lager. It didn't take us long to get into the politics of Czechoslovakia and what we both thought of the Russians. He was hesitant to tell me that his father was the ousted president, and the new man in charge was a Russian puppet.

Our conversation was influenced a little with the amount of beer we had, so I decided it would be best to work on this straight-talking young man tomorrow morning. As I got into bed Lenka sleepily told me good night and could I help in getting breakfast in the morning, and then help prepare the Sunday roast for our guests.

At breakfast while serving the group their first cup of coffee, they all collectively apologized for one of the group's rude behavior towards me last night. I brushed it off by telling them I have already forgotten the incident, and adding that there is no purpose in keeping the issue going. They seemed to agree and liked the philosophy of letting it go.

When Lenka and I sat down to join the group in having breakfast Antonin asked teasingly, "Is the kitchen help allowed to join the esteem guests in this establishment?"

Lenka was fuming and did not know Antonin was being funny until I said, "With the esteem guests privileged to have the far more likable kitchen help join them, an extra fare will be placed on their rooms as the time spent with the help is a valuable addition. The charges may be so great that the esteemed guests may have to wash up and thus making them the kitchen help and the past kitchen help as their superiors."

Everyone roared with laughter and that would set up the start of an association that would last for many months through the good and the bad.

After breakfast we all went with Lenka to walk her dog. The walk was a good workout through the forest and the hills behind the hotel. We all would eventually talk to one another one-on-one and never noticed that we were gone for a little over three hours.

When we got back close to the hotel we saw a police car parked outside the hotel. All of us were shocked to see the police this far from Prague.

I suggested, "Maybe you all should go, leaving me in the forest, since a foreigner in your group may cause trouble."

They all agreed, why muddy the water with someone from outside the country? As they got near the hotel two policemen got out of their little squad car. One was a plain clothes officer with a limp. He looked from a distance like the man I broke the leg of on my first assignment. After an hour the two policemen left and I went inside the hotel.

Lenka said, "The rude boy from last night went to the police station this morning to report a foreigner was staying here. We assured them that we were all Czechs. He also described to them what you look like. The man in the suit said they have been looking for a man who looked liked you Ludwig. Let's talk

173

about this after lunch; everyone will have to help in the kitchen now that it is past lunchtime."

Everyone was looking at me in the kitchen trying to figure out who I was. My expression had to be one of seriousness as not to telegraph a person of someone who was careless or self-aggrandizing. This group was way too astute to accept a foolish fellow.

After lunch we were all sitting at a large extended table having coffee, and one could sense an inquisition was on the horizon. Studying everyone it was evident Antonin was going to start the proceedings.

It wasn't long before he asked, "Is your name Ludwig?"

"It is one of them."

Everyone's reaction was telling. Lenka was the most expressive as she tried to speak and couldn't form a coherent sentence. All of the young men just stared in disbelief.

Antonin finally said, "Tell us please who you are and your purpose for being in our country?"

"My name is Malcolm McLeod, and I am here to offer assistance in the form of money and planning to your cause."

Lenka asked, "How many names do you have and what is your real name given to you at birth, I have a right to know after what we have been through. Where were you born?"

"My real name is William Wright. I am an American agent helping important people go to the West."

Everyone was really taken back in having an American agent in front of them who was not hiding who he was and wanted to help in any way he could.

Antonin then asked after a few moments, "How much funding are you willing to give us and how would you handle the protest?"

"I have 75,000 Korunas for you today and when you protest remember the authorities are filming you. You need to have your own film crew to catch any hostile activity by the Russians. I will take the film to the West and expose the real intent of the opposition through various news networks."

I was asked to prove there was that amount of money for their cause. I left to go to my room and returned to give the funds to Antonin. He was pleased and got up to hug me as a tear rolled down his cheek.

He said, "We do have someone who cares about us outside our prison borders. We do accept your help in making our country free once again."

Lenka asked, "Who do you work for and why help us and not other Soviet Bloc countries who need just as much help?"

"I work for two agencies and cannot divulge any more for your own protection and for mine."

"I must warn you that the police and military will visit this hotel again tonight and take apart the place looking for me. I am the most wanted person in Czechoslovakia as of now. Someone needs to go to the main road and see if a blockade has been set up around this place.

"If I leave now I can travel through the forest and work my way around the perimeter. You have to say that no one else was here especially me or they will interrogate all of you for days to obtain any piece of information. You will not satisfy their thirst for information."

Lenka immediately took her dog for a walk and to see if my suspicions were right. She was back within 10 minutes and shaken up as the two policemen seemed to be waiting for someone back up at the main intersection.

Lenka suggested I leave by the road that would get me away from the area quicker.

I told her, "If I did that the police and military would take you all in for helping a suspected spy. If I left through the forest then they would never know I was here. You will have to rake my tracts leading to the forest, especially the bike tracks. Take your money and hide it under some leftover food in one of the ovens. I really must go now and hope to see you all again. One of you will have to move to my room and spread out dirty clothes as to make it look like it was your room."

I quickly gathered my gear and left pushing the bike through the forest. After working my way around to the right of the area for several hours or until it was getting dark, I was on the main road to Prague. I made it to the Gypsy village and parked the bike in the rear of the house I use as far in the rear of the village as possible. Topol came to get me to stay with them tonight. I was just in time to join him and his family for supper. He sat me next to his daughter and she was so close we were touching each other at the hips. With being on the end of the bench, I couldn't move away as it was getting uncomfortably warm with her touching me as her father looked on.

After we ate and still at the table he asked his daughter to translate.

I said, "The police are looking for me and they know I am in the Prague area. They have called in the military to assist with their search. I am wanted for espionage and the murder of 10 soldiers according to the secret police."

Topol asked, "You espionage person, no. The murder of 10 people, no. Are you not the man to do this, 10 soldiers."

"No, not that many. Your daughter must forget about me as I will always be running away from the authorities."

He looked at his daughter and said, "What he say is right, you must forget him."

Topol's daughter went to her room in the back of the cabin. At least that was a problem solved for now. We planned out how we were going to get to Plzen tomorrow. The consensus was we would have to go south away from Prague, and then head back west to Plzen.

When the strategy session was over I excused myself and went to my assigned cabin for some much needed sleep, and time to contemplate my next move. Around midnight and in a confused state of grogginess, I was awakened by the door's hinges squeaking as Topol's daughter was entering my room.

She crawled into my warm bed, wanting me to embrace her. All I could think of was if the oversized king of the Gypsies caught us I would never be heard of again regardless of the circumstances. On the other hand, what if I said no and then the frostiness set in, the protective father may have thought we were together anyway last night.

I gave in and we spent the night together, then Leila left as the sun was breaking. I waited until all the lights were on in the big man's house before going over to get this over with. No one spoke for the longest time as we ate breakfast.

Finally the daughter asked if she could say something. I was about to make a run for it and looked to see if my bike was still parked in the back of the camp. Sweat beads were now forming on my forehead as I found it hard to swallow whatever I was eating at that precise time.

She said, "Papa, I know you and mama are right that Ludwig and I should not go out together until he gets a real job where he will be home all the time."

I couldn't stop shaking like it was cold in here, even though it was warm. Her words brought great relief to my state of mind, but not to my nerves. Topol was reverent in his reply and I was as quiet as a church mouse. I let it just lay there without comment.

I told Topol as I got up from the table, "You will be arrested if you are caught with me. I need for you to stay around here and be ready in case a driver is needed at a later date. I will say goodbye and leave you with money for any future transportation, which may be sooner than you think. We need to cancel the trip to Plzen for now."

I left to go back to see Lenka and get the update on what happened when I left. The roads were clear all the way to the hotel, except for people cycling to work on the edge of Prague. I parked the bike on the edge of the village behind a cafe and walked to the hotel, approaching it from the front as a worker would do. I entered through the kitchen's back door by the trash cans after looking inside them to make it appear that they may need emptying. Lenka was surprised to see me and told me everything that went on after I left.

She said, "It wasn't long after I left, the military came to the hotel with a truck load of soldiers. Most of them were instructed to go into the forest. The two policemen and two Russian officers came in and looked into every room. They then started interrogating each of us in separate rooms, about the person who was here last night and was now nowhere to be seen. In the end they apologized for the disruption and left. Antonin, along with his friends, are meeting at a cafe near the Plzen town center and asked me to tell you to meet them there if you came back."

The next morning it was eerily quiet and still, strange that no birds could be heard. I went up to my room and hid the rest of the dollars along with my papers and gun under the carpet and floor boards. I felt something was not right and told Lenka I will be back soon. A note was under her pillow on what to do if she hasn't heard from me in one week.

Outside I poured one trash can into another and took the full one to the bottom of the drive. As I got to the bike a police car pulled into the hotel's drive and stopped. An army truck pulled in to drop off soldiers as other soldiers came out of the forest to get into the truck. I had to wait until they were all gone or in the forest before starting the machine.

It was imperative to get as far away as possible so they could not connect me to the hotel and more importantly to Lenka. I managed to arrive in Plzen and run into Antonin and his colleagues. They were inside the cafe and asked me to join them for lunch. Antonin was about to tell me of the activity last night at the hotel, when a half dozen soldiers came in for something to eat. They were all Russians and started to tease us about our hair and the way we were dressed. The more we ignored them the ruder they became. A waitress asked them to leave as they were upsetting the customers.

The biggest Russian got up from his chair and brought his fist back to strike her. I reacted and got to her in time to stop his hand from hitting her in the face. After grabbing the flying arm and pulling it down and sweeping him off his feet, he hit the floor with a loud thud. The others were stunned that he was left helpless in a few seconds. The waitress escorted us out to the back door while the soldiers helped their friend up, and told us to hurry to get away. I told them to wait here while I led the soldiers away by going to the opposite side of the road in front of the cafe.

They spotted me and chased me through small cobblestone roads. I could hear their army truck closing in. After heading towards the opposite direction of the truck's noise and losing them, I then headed into a direction where I thought the bike was parked. It wasn't long before I was at a dead end and started back to find another route.

I was thinking how was it that a chivalrous act could be the end of this assignment, what was I thinking when the assignment should have trumped everything else, no matter the consequences. At least the young lady was safe even though I may not be if I do not get to my motorbike. I was now running low of breath with every step.

# Chapter 9

## Bory: AKA Gory Prison Hospital

Hearing the truck getting closer and running around a corner, something hit me over the head; it felt like a sledgehammer that made me drop to the pavement.

I was groggy as they threw me into an army truck. The big Russian embarrassed at being thrown was kicking me as I lay on the truck's floor. We were going about 40 miles an hour when I grabbed his boot, twisting his leg causing him to follow his leg; hence, I was able to kick him out the back of the truck. He hit the tarmac headfirst that made a sound like a melon hitting the road.

That was the last thing I remembered for several days. They must have worked me over pretty good in the truck. I had the wherewithal to fake waking up until I could survey the situation while lying on a table. I had a feeling I was in the infamous Bory Prison. The room had bars on the door painted white and turning a yellowish color with the thick paint chipping away. This room resembled an antiquated hospital room with blood-stained, surgical type tin wash basins. My clothes were soaked with dried blood and I must have lost at least a pint of blood.

Voices were heard reverberating off stone walls. After an hour or so an orderly looking lady came in to check my pulse, leaving the door open.

After pushing myself to get up and run for it, my legs gave way which seemed strange. I was shackled to a bolt in the floor that caused me to trip. The large lady called for someone to help get me back on the cold steel slab. A soldier started to hit me as I turned my face and said in German dummkopf. He was astounded I was still in a fighting mood. He must have known what it meant as he threw me back on the cold, hard narrow steel table. Or maybe they needed me to be awake.

A medical-type officer with a white coat came in as the other soldier looked on to make sure I was not going to be a problem. He said something in Czech.

I replied in German, "Nicht verstehen (I do not understand). You have to speak German if you want answers."

I assumed his German was lacking when he started to speak in broken English. "You have had a nasty accident; we are taking care for you. We treat foreigners too good. Where are you from, not Germany; you look too well, good shape and fed. You say in sleep you are British, a Malcolm McLeod, named after grandfather. Someone here to see you, nice Russian colonel, take you to better place to rest."

After blacking out again I woke up to see and feel a soldier slapping me with a glove. I grabbed the glove in my teeth and spit it on the floor.

He leaned over close to my ear and said in perfect English, "When the general gets through with you I will finish you off for good."

A general was now in the room and asked everyone to leave him. After the door was closed, he shouted at the colonel to go away as the evil colonel was watching from the hall.

He said, "We know all about you, you are a British or American agent who has caused our government a lot of pain over the past year. You have murdered 10 of our soldiers; no, it is now 11 after you threw one from the truck. We have ways of making you pay for the soldiers' lives you have wasted.

"Let me start with you telling me how you were able to get four lots of our top scientists and their off springs out of the German Republic and Czechoslovakia. You will tell me now or later. We would like all of the names of the traitors that help you."

"I am not a British agent, only a shy student."

He roared with laughter as the room filled up with prison hospital staff to see what was happening. He told them what was said and they all joined him in the laughter. He then ordered a pot of tea to be made with a jug of hot water on the side. He was strange and didn't say anything else until the tea arrived. He asked the orderly to prop me up so I could sip the tea, then leave and to get everyone away from this ward.

He bent over and said, "Scream when I pour the scolding hot water on the floor and answer, "I will tell you everything."

I was in a quandary as to what he was up to with me still in chains. I screamed and did as he told me to do. Now what is going to happen next with this guy, he must be bonkers?

He leaned over like he were going to kiss my neck and said, "If I get you out of here will you get me and my family over to a Western country?"

"Your name please, general."

"Senja."

"I know about you, and that you are suspected of taking bribes."

"That is not true, another general wants my rank. We go in one week from today; I have to collect some important papers."

"One week from today I will be gone from here."

The Czech General roared again with laughter and said, "You are too funny, no one has ever left this place alive. The grounds are full of ashes where grass cannot grow. You are the funniest spy I have ever met; we can be friends in America."

"Okay General, what is your name again and if I do get out you will have to meet me with your family at the entrance to Charles University, agreed. Before you go what day is it? Meet me seven days from now."

As he was leaving he said it was Monday and his name was Senja. It couldn't be that I was out for a week without food. I then noticed needle marks on both arms. They must have fed me by tubes. The oversized male and female orderlies came in to probably work me over again. The big man told me the colonel wanted me up and ready to travel this afternoon.

I was ordered to get my clothes on along with a large stuffed army coat they gave me. The orderly informed me that I was to be taken to Leipzig to face a court marshal and then would be placed in front of a firing squad.

The colonel showed up as I finished a bowl of foul-tasting gritty gruel. The texture was like undercooked oatmeal and tasted of strong soy. The orderly dragged me out of the room and out to a waiting army truck. After throwing me in the back on the floor and shackling me to a metal bench, the colonel asked for the keys to the shackles. I was left in the back with the tarp pulled down and latched.

We were gone for about half an hour when the truck pulled over. The colonel was alone and unlocked the chains as he pointed a pistol at my head. He walked me up front to the driver's door and motioned me to get over.

We took off towards the place I crossed over and was told to let him know where the first pouch of money was buried. I could not believe the hypnotic plan was working as I was pretending to pass out.

He hit me in the face with the back of his gloved hand, which smelled of petrol to wake me up. I motioned for him to pull over as I spotted the crossed limbs by the side of the road. Pointing the gun again at my head, he ordered me to slide out of the truck past the steering wheel. I slid to the ground where he grabbed me as I slumped down and almost hit the tarmac.

The colonel handed me a shovel from behind his seat, and I was told to walk to where the money was buried. It was easy to spot the marker and that's where I was told to dig. When I got to the dead rabbit, he pulled me backwards out of the way to make sure a weapon wasn't with the money. He stuck his gloved hand into the rabbit when he saw the pouch. The smell was overpowering as he made a big ugh and threw the glove away as he stuffed the loot inside his jacket.

He pushed me forward as I pretended to fall and groan out loud with pain. He then gently pushed me forward again towards the other buried money. When we got to the partial deer carcass over the foxhole, he wanted to know if there was another dead animal with money stuffed inside of it. I nodded yes; he then ordered me to get down and bring the money out. I dug around until I felt the shovel hit the pouch. I held my nose while I fumbled around and then used both hands to pretend to pull out the cash.

With my right hand I picked the pistol up and now with my index finger on the trigger with the cash with the left hand. I pulled the cash out as he lowered his gun to take the pouch from me. The horrid Russian made the biggest mistake of his life when his hand came over my left shoulder.

I brought the gun out and he could sense it was too late for him to bring his weapon up, he knew it was all over. He started talking loud with lots of gibberish as I shot him in the forehead.

He lay dead as I started stripping him of the money and his possessions, along with his whole uniform as he wasn't going to need them anymore; and maybe they may come in handy sometime later. I then stuffed him in the same hole under limbs with the deer carcass on top again. I drove the army truck back to the Plzen to get my bike, leaving the truck in back of the cafe.

Arriving at Lenka's hotel, I needed a hot bath and to have her wash the saddlebags, money and uniform while washing the stench from my body; she never asked what happened, she knew. Her parents were due to arrive in the next couple of days. She brought me a cup of tea while I was in the bath. She gasped as she noticed a lot of new bruises on my chest and back along with needle marks. Before Lenka went down to the kitchen to warm up some soup, she wanted to tell me something very important.

She said, "Antonin and his friends stopped here a week ago and told me what happened. They heard that you were taken to Bory Prison and how brave you were; and also stupid to take on those Russian soldiers just to help a woman from being hit. I said to them you are certainly not stupid just a little careless. Oh Billy, when are you going to stop what you do?"

My stay ended up with her for five days as her parents were delayed, most likely by weather. On the sixth day I gathered up all of the money that was now washed and dried. I had to see Topol to change some dollars into Crowns to pay for another year's hotel bill. I needed 5,000 Korunas for Andrea and the same for the hotel. Plus, I needed another 10,000 for the student fund.

Topol, when told of the plan, was not happy with having a Czech general in his taxi; but he would do the job for 100 Yankee dollars. I would have to make sure that it was not a trap by getting to the pickup point early to watch for anything unusual.

I left to see if Andrea was home and knocked on her door. She was so happy to see me and invited me in to meet her parents. We escaped to her bedroom where I handed over her year's wages. She pretended not to want it and then acted like it was too much. As I was leaving she walked down with me to ask a few questions.

We went to a cafe where it was safe to talk. Andrea told me she was now the concierge at the Hotel Jalta and wondered if I would like to stay there tonight. She still works for the secret police as a call girl when a Westerner is staying at the hotel. She wanted to know all about the last year and if I was married to the London school teacher. I told her yes I was married and am very happy. We talked the night away and I had to stay at the hotel because of the time. I asked her where a safe phone was so I could call someone in the West.

She took me down to the hotel basement where the secret police and Russian headquarters were. We entered the Russian office where I called the ASA headquarters and told the first sergeant to meet me tomorrow afternoon. We went back upstairs to have one more drink. Andrea asked if I wanted her to go to bed with me. I told her I was tortured by a Russian in Bory Prison and was still out of commission.

The next morning I was awakened with room service bringing in breakfast, with Andrea following close behind. She saw the many bruises and understood why I was out of commission. She talked as I ate the delicious food, with her divulging even more secret information on the new town the Russians were building 30 miles away.

I asked Andrea, "Is this room safe to talk in? I am worried that someone will hear you and report you to the police."

"Yes, it is safe, I turned the machine off. You wanted to know the general in charge of the new town. I copied his file for you. When will I see you again Billy?"

"I may be back in a few days, before I go is it possible to work out of the hotel next year and use it as my base, or is it too dangerous for you?"

"Yes it is; I will make sure you will not be discovered."

"Thank you Andrea, I will see more of you in the future then. Now I have to get dressed and be somewhere soon."

I put on the new uniform of the colonel I'd recently killed. Andrea had already had it dry cleaned. It was very winkled from the wash Lenka gave it, but now it looked pretty spiffy.

After getting to the university early and observing the area for several hours, the general showed up with a young girl and a young man. The general looked frightened when he saw me.

I asked him, "What is wrong? You look terrified General."

He said, "Malcolm, you are one crazy spy. I thought my time was up when all I could see was a Russian colonel coming towards me. The hospital told me you were taken out of there by a Russian officer to be transported to Moscow. The uniform belonged to that officer, no. When we get to America you must tell me how you are the first person to have escaped from Bory and then becoming a Russian colonel."

"The nice colonel let me borrow it for a while."

Topol showed up as we started towards him; he was about to drive away until I shouted out to him it was me.

Topol said, "You have gone too far this time, English, impersonating a Russian officer again, they will shoot you."

"I thought I was family Topol. Take these three in your taxi and I will follow with the motorbike to guard you. When we get close to the area I will pass your taxi and have you stop at a place where we will need to be."

Three hours later Topol was on his way back home as we were at the path and going towards the border. I led the way past the smelly deer carcass and now the smelly Russian body. I looked back to see the three of them holding their noses. Just before the border I gave the general $1,000 to get him started in America. When we crossed under the barb wire, the team came forward to help us.

Summerall asked, "Who are these people Wright? I don't recall any orders for you bringing assets back."

"Sir, this is General Senja and his family. The general will work with you on information concerning the Russian project at Bozi Dar. I have to go now and will see you as planned or sooner, will call you from the same number as yesterday."

"Wait a damn minute Wright, that number you called from was the number of the Russian headquarters in Czechoslovakia. What is going on?"

"Sorry sir, I can't be late for the meeting in Prague."

I heard him say to the first sergeant as I was leaving, "Do you want to go help him and find out what he is doing, sergeant?"

"No sir, believe me, he doesn't want my help. I would be in the way and shudder to think what he might get up to in the next two months."

I looked back quickly to see all of them shake their heads as they walked into the forest.

It was time to go back straight to the Areal Hotel to spend a few days even though Lenka's parents were probably back from their skiing holiday. Outside the hotel were the bicycles of Antonin and his followers. I opened the barn door to put the bike expecting to see the parents' car. No car, which caused me to be a little curious.

Entering the hotel through the kitchen and back door, Lenka rushed over to give me a hug and started to cry. She was told I was taken to the big prison and was never seen again.

I was led to the lounge where the five young men looked as if they were seeing a ghost. I gave Antonin another 10,000 Korunas. He was speechless as he took the cash.

Everyone was just staring and finally Antonin said, "How did you get out?"

"It wasn't easy. Lenka helped by contacting someone that needed my help, a general no less. By the way, the oversized Russian will not be striking any more women in the future."

They looked stunned at that revelation. We partied all night. Lenka's parents will be in tomorrow and the boys are going to Plzen.

The next morning while Lenka and I got breakfast for everyone, she let me know how the boys thought what I did was something they could never do. She told me "Now they want you to help plan the uprising from here, as their headquarters are here. My parents may be worried but I know they will understand and help them." At that moment the parents pulled in front of the hotel. Lenka rushed out as I added two more eggs to the bowl to be scrambled.

I was peeling potatoes when Mrs. Dagmar came into the kitchen. She smiled as if she knew what Lenka and I were up to. After a hug she welcomed me back to the Areal Hotel. Mr. Dagmar came in and shook my hand and also welcomed me back. We all had breakfast together after the boys carried the luggage upstairs.

While having coffee Antonin asked Mr. Dagmar if they could use the hotel for the headquarters of the uprising. Of course he balked and was worried he may be caught and closed down. The discussion went on and on with Lenka getting upset with her father, and accused him of being unreasonable. His response was a very resounding no. He heard from everyone except me and wanted to know what I thought about the request.

I said, "Let's look at the pros and cons of having the meetings held here. The only pro was it is remote. Can anyone give me another favorable reason it should be here? No I didn't think so. The cons are this place has no vantage point to watch for approaching police.

"It would be a trap as you well know from past experience. There is an abandoned farmhouse on top of a hill half way to Plzen on the curve of the main road. You can see in all directions and especially the road. Set up your headquarters upstairs and you would have an escape route out the back."

Everyone agreed that being remote and having a visual advantaged was needed. Lenka's parents were relieved. The only consolation was that I had become a member and the logistics officer.

Later that day we all biked to the farmhouse 20 miles away that was used in the past to sleep in on a previous assignment. Lenka and I were on the motorbike, scouted the road, and waited for the group to show up.

We explored the house and barns to see if anything could used in our headquarters, and to find the best lookout point.

While we waited Lenka said, "My father had a look of relief when you said the hotel was too vulnerable to have our headquarters there. We can clean this place up and hold our meetings in the room where the sun is most prevalent as we will need heat to keep us warm. When are you leaving again?"

"I am not sure. This assignment will take another eight weeks to complete. No one knows what is in the future for me."

The rest of the group pulled in and parked their bicycles inside the house. We all watched the road from the vantage point Lenka picked out. It was settled we would meet here next weekend, and after a couple of hours all of us took off to head back to our homes. Lenka and I arrived back at the hotel to walk her dog and prepare the evening meal. Her parents were still sleeping as we crept around doing chores, so they could relax when they woke up.

The next morning before taking off to stay at the Hotel Jalta, I gave Mr. Dagmar the money to keep my room reserved for another year.

For the next eight weeks we all met on weekends on the anti-establishment and anti-Soviet Union protest with me going to the new town worksite during the week to get information on how many bunkers, silos and the size of the runway, which our U2 could pick up anyway. The Jalta was much more convenient to stay in from Monday to Friday than the Botanika. The weeks dragged by with watching a building site most days.

In the eighth week, a day before Charles University was due to close for the spring semester break, I went to see Professor Ivo. He recognized me from the times I was supposed to have been an exchange student. He was solemn and looked downtrodden, probably from hearing the chatter about the planned student uprising. He wouldn't stop to listen to me, especially when I mentioned that it would be a good idea if some of the faculty helped lead the protest from the front of the procession.

He stopped in his tracts when I said, "Leos sends his best, doctor."

Professor Ivo asked hesitantly, "Where is Leos? I have inquired several times with no luck of getting any information. His parents must be worried. How do you know where he is?"

"Leos is attending Cambridge University and his parents are working in America. I took him and his parents across to the West at different intervals from Prague and Leipzig. In Washington, there is a rumor that you want to lecture in America."

"I have much to lose, not taking into account being thrown in some cold gulag in Russia. There is nothing anyone can do except flee this prison like country. I will leave one day when the opportunity arises. I knew something was up the day you so rudely walked in to my class last January a year ago uninvited. I never did think there was much to you that first chance meeting. Now I have second thoughts about my ability to judge someone by their actions. You must leave me to ponder what must be done in the coming weeks. Where can I reach you if I am need of your services?"

I walked out without answering him to go back to get my bike. I thought how selfish he was, knowing his students could be harmed while he cowered in the corner of his precious classroom.

It was now the end of March and I was due to leave in less than a week for London and my flat thanks to Uncle Sam. The last strategy meeting was scheduled for this weekend, and me leaving for the border as soon as it was over. Lenka was prepared for my departure and knew the next time she saw me I could be a married man. Somehow it didn't matter that week as she treated me like a king. The assignment was so far a success. I still had close to $20,000 in cash from this job and another 10,000 pounds stashed away in London with some loose change for luxuries.

I was two days away from meeting Summerall and the team at the border when news came in that the troops being used to quell the protest were from other Soviet Bloc countries.

Antonin and his group were here at Lenka's hotel getting ready for the march. We all assembled at noon to go over last-minute plans.

I advised the group to stop the protest and wait until the troops went back to their countries since the Russians did not have to use their own soldiers. I explained that if a march never took place then the embarrassment would be against the Soviets. They thought that was an excellent ploy and left immediately to try to stop as many students as they could from showing up at Saturday's uprising.

# Chapter 10

## Bullets and Demands

Early next morning, it was Good Friday, and I left Lenka at the hotel door waving goodbye as I drove towards the border to meet my team at noon. I had an extra hour or two built in for unknown obstacles; however, with the army and police gearing up for the uprising, this part of the Czech Republic was void of any military. Helicopters were being used to fly low over the border area, which was causing some consternation.

I stopped short of my destination by about a mile and watched two choppers as they went away south, which gave me time to go back to the road and get closer to the marker. I kept the forest as cover between darting out and back in, which was time-consuming. I finally made it to the path and made my way to cross over. When I got to the fence the two choppers were just flying over at treetop level; they passed over me by less than 40 feet as I waited for them to get out of sight. I pushed the bike under the barb wire as a third helicopter joined the other two by trailing them a mile behind, which was really bad luck.

I cranked the bike up and ran for cover just as the chopper let off a barrage of bullets, hitting the rear tire. I grabbed the saddlebags, threw them over my shoulder, and left the bike with the rear tire smoking. I ran as fast as these legs would take me. I had to run at least two kilometers to be in West Germany. Now all three helicopters were overhead as I ran. Good thing the forest was thick or they would have certainly gunned me down.

Bullets were still being shot towards the back of me as limbs were hitting the ground and getting closer and closer. I stopped and shielded myself behind a tree just as a chopper flew over. I could see a soldier with his legs outside holding a machine gun. I shot my pistol towards him with one of my bullets hitting one of his legs. The chopper hastily pulled away along with the other two.

By the time I thought I was in the clear a helicopter landed 100 yards in front of me in a clearing. I know that chopper was in West Germany territory and probably was a gun-happy Russian pilot making a stupid decision without thinking.

I quickly covered myself with limbs and pine straw and lay prone or as flat as I could. Just as two soldiers walked past me by about three feet, I jumped up and pulled one over to me by his neck and put him into a choke hold and placed my pistol against his head.

The other pilot or soldier didn't know what to do as he was itching to end this now.

I quietly muttered, "Uhn uhn," and motioned for him to get on the ground by pointing my gun downward. He dropped his weapon and waited for me to make a mistake as his rifle was still close to him. I motioned again for him to throw his weapon farther away. He picked the rifle up by its stock as his hand reached for the trigger; I shot him in the forehead.

By the time he fell forward my team was on me, I never heard the bus drive up. Summerall ordered me to let the other man go as he was almost dead from the chokehold.

Summerall felt the soldier's pulse and said, "It's a miracle, Wright brought us a live one for the first time; well, barely alive."

The other two choppers started to land to help their comrades. I picked up one of the rifles and shot the rotor blades of both helicopters with two shots.

They decided to wobble off towards the border and get the hell out of here.

Summerall shouted, "Wright, we may be in Czech Territory, but your actions could start a world conflict with the USSR. I have to protest your actions."

"Protest all you want, I will not be shot or captured while I wait until you have this area surveyed. Do you really believe the Russian choppers cared if they were in West Germany; no, they were bent on reprisal to having one of their comrades shot back across the border."

The first sergeant quickly joined the fray by saying, "We can go over if we were in Czech territory back at our base. What do we do with the dead soldier and the live soldier? The helicopter will have to be dealt with."

I answered him as the old man went silent, "Since this is my doing, I am taking over this problem. Do you agree with that Major or is this your baby now?"

Summerall raised his open hands in a given in jesting and saying, "It's yours Major Wright."

"Thank you, sir. Now listen everyone, the first thing we do is contact the Army civil engineers from the Hof Air Base to quickly survey this area and take the helicopter to a base in Nuremberg. The dead soldier, we take to a funeral director in the town of Hof. This alive soldier will gladly be a friend and will now officially defect, especially if we go get his family today."

Summerall couldn't wait to wade in and point to a flaw in my summation when he asked, "How in the hell can you say this soldier will defect, you haven't asked him."

At that moment I grabbed the soldier by his collar and turned him away from us and shoved him towards the border and Czechoslovakia.

He dropped to his knees and in broken English said, "I stay here."

Without knowing the Czech language, Summerall asked in English, "Are you sure? We will let you go home."

He answered the old man in a long, begging like diatribe that no one could decipher. The soldier then started speaking in Russian, and as the first sergeant was fluent in Russian, he took over the interrogation.

After the seemingly endless conversation with the soldier, the first sergeant finally gave us the extent of his pleading.

The soldier said he has a Czech uniform on but he is actually a Russian noncommissioned officer impersonating a Czech private. Only for border patrol duties, to have the NATO forces think no Russians are here. However, he does have a wife in the Plzen area that needs to be brought over. She is a Czech citizen living in an off base facility close to the army air field outside the main town. "Wright, you may want to go back and get her today as we are not that far from there now. We will wait here until you get back."

"That will not be possible sergeant as my motorcycle was shot out from under me and have no way of getting there today. Wait a minute… a couple miles away I did stash a Czech army staff jeep on a previous assignment. I need a photograph of the lady and where she will be today or tonight. Go to our previous crossings and create a diversion from this area. Take the dead soldier and lay him next to the border fence in another area so he can be seen from the air by scouting chopper. Get this helicopter out of here now and have the placed surveyed so I may be vindicated. Be back here this evening to take us out of here."

After getting the photo from the soldier's wallet, and one of his dog tags along with an address, I started to take off after I threw the saddlebags to the first sergeant.

The old man noticed when I turned to go there was blood on the back of my jacket. I ignored him calling me back and took off. All the time spent walking and running back to the Czech border and then to the main road, I thought *this is madness, Plzen of all places.* At least the base was this side of the town.

It was going to be dark in two to three hours where time was going to be a huge problem. The stashed jeep had better be there or it will be impossible to cross back over today. With having second thoughts, I should have told the team no. It is too late now, what a mess. I couldn't believe the luck of the lady who was about to be taken to the West. The jeep was still there. I made my way towards Plzen and found the place where Russian dependents were housed.

I was still in my Russian uniform when I knocked on the wife's door. She let me in and asked in

Czechoslovakian was her husband okay or why are you here if he has not had an accident.

I closed the door and asked her in English."Speak English? I do not speak your language. You must come with me now to see your husband. He has had an accident with the helicopter crashing."

She didn't answer or say anything as she grabbed her heavy coat. She got into the jeep and I drove as fast as I could back to the path through the Bohemian Forest. I couldn't risk her being told she was going to defect and wanting to think it over. We got back to the road marker, and I took a chance by driving through the trees as fast as the situation allowed me. It was starting to get dark when the jeep slid into a tree and we had to walk the rest of the way. She pulled her hand out of my tight grasp and stooped and did not want to go any farther.

I said, "Come, your husband's helicopter has crashed in West Germany and that is where I am taking you. She started to cry and I couldn't take any more time to console her. I showed her the photograph and his dog tags and told her I was an American sent to get her. I will leave you here if you do not hurry, and you will never see your husband again; do you understand?"

She nodded and we took off running. We crossed the border and ran to where the helicopter crashed. It was gone, but a squad of combat engineers was there surveying the crash site by flashlight. The chopper really didn't crash; it was just sat down hard. The lieutenant in charge of the surveying squad was scared out of his wits when I ran out of the trees in a Russian uniform.

He said, "Christ almighty what is this, who in the hell are you?"

"I am an American ASA agent coming in from the Soviet Bloc. My name is Wright; my team will be here soon to extract us."

"Yeah, yeah, I was told you may be showing up. You scared the crap out of me running towards us like you did. They told me you are about the craziest person I will ever meet and they are right."

"They are wrong Lieutenant; I am just a good old country boy like yourself. Is this site in West Germany or is it part of the Czech Republic?"

"Yeah, sure you are. I know, I don't want to get to know you. Yes, it is in West Germany by about 400 yards, give or take a yard or two."

I turned my attention to the soldier's wife and finally asked her, did she want to go to the West? She nervously answered that her husband talked about escaping to the West many times.

The bus drove up as it was too dark for the survey crew to continue. They were able to get close coordinates with so many of their crew here to help. Captain Summerall went to speak to the lieutenant about his findings with the survey team looking in my direction, and telling them something that made them shake their heads.

Standing by the bus Summerall said, "Wright the lieutenant said you took a few years off of his life and suggested you need some quiet time. You are lucky the site is in friendly territory."

"What makes you think I would take the fall for this international mishap, Major Summerall."

With that remark the team members started to laugh. While all of this was going on, the wife ran up to embrace her husband as he stepped off the team bus. They then came over to me when Summerall finished his half- baked apology, and both said thanks for helping the wife get across today. It was strange that they never kissed or shed a tear with being in a free country that they said they always wanted, something was missing.

The first sergeant said, "Wright, we all had bets you were not coming back today and probably would be apprehended. Do you ever say no to an assignment? We are glad you took it anyway, you crazy SOB."

"First sergeant, I have to give a briefing to three generals in a few days on a beach in Florida. Meet my fiancé tomorrow in London and take her on the trip. Time is closing in on me right now. You are correct; I do find it hard to decline a mission. Whatever time we get back this evening we have to have a briefing so I can drive to Frankfurt in the morning. Now tell me, did the diversion work with the bait at the other crossing area?"

Summerall jumped into the discussion and suggested we leave all of the talk now until the briefing. We headed back to Bad Aibling and I went to the back of the bus to get some sleep. I was awakened when the bus pulled into the base and in front of the mess hall where the kitchen crew was waiting for us.

After we all ate, the first sergeant escorted the two defectors to where they were going to sleep for the night, and then it was time for the briefing in the ASA conference room.

I asked the first sergeant, "Have a doctor look at me when the briefing was over in my bedroom. He will need something to fix two or three bullet wounds that grazed me at the border. I seem to need to scratch several places on my back, and it's driving me crazy."

This briefing would span the last three months including notes taken from General Senja's briefing last month. I was given a copy of that briefing to either concur with the testimony or put in my own interpretation of the actual events that took place. The generals' report seemed pretty close to the truth, except for him taking the credit for helping me escape, typical general taking all the credit.

Summerall instructed me to not generalize, but to report everything, including what may seem insignificant. He needed the Czech general's briefing validated with a signature from me before starting this session.

Summerall added, "The answer to your question at the pickup point, yes the ploy or diversion worked. We were covered up with a Soviet-style cavalry, a squadron of helicopters with troops inside or what we now use in South Vietnam as a rapid deployment force. In finishing, the Soviet exercise was a gift as we monitored their procedure, which was added to our report.

I thanked him for that and started with the psychotherapist training that Bartholomew administered to me in London, and then to the crossing the Czech border with the team's help in the second week of January.

Summerall interrupted. He wanted the hard and gory bits, not a preamble.

"Alright sir, you asked for it. After leaving you at the border, I set a trap on the path to the main road for the purpose of getting away from a would be captor. Arriving at the safe house halfway to Prague, I joined a team of university students who were engaged in an anti-establishment protest. I managed to gain their confidence and became a part of their team.

"The students and I would eventually meet up in the town of Plzen. An incident happened where I was arrested, and on the way to Bory Prison a Russian soldier fell out of the back of a speeding transport and was killed. I was beaten and tortured for five to seven days. I was shackled to a metal antiquated operating table in the hospital section of the prison with my feet chained to a bolt on the floor.

"A hypothetical story was planted in my mind by Doctor Bartholomew; somehow it worked as a Russian colonel took the bait and was eventually terminated beside the forest path used for getting in and out of Czechoslovakia. General Sejna visited me before I was taken out of the place by an evil colonel, and we agreed to meet in Prague in a week. I returned to the safe house to rest up and meet again with the students.

"Wrapped around this time I met with two of contacts in Prague and went over items of transport, and the news of a new Russian town being built, along with visiting the construction site numerous times.

"The hotel I used in Prague is the Jalta where the CIA also has two rooms, and is available most of the year. The concierge is a contact and now a close female friend. The students agreed to wait until the foreign troops left the country and they would then continue with their protest."

Summerall dismissed us and drove me to where a medic and a nurse were waiting in my bedroom across the hall from our new guest. After all of my shirts and jacket was off the doctor asked me to lie on the bed face down. The old man, seeing three or four bullets in my back said, "You can't be operated on here, you have to go to the Munich Hospital."

"No sir, I don't have the time. These two can do the job; anyway, the saddle bag took the sting out of the shots. See you in the morning for an early breakfast sir."

The medic ordered the CO to leave so they could fix me up. The doctor instructed the nurse to give me a sedative.

She said, "There isn't any."

"Take the whiskey bottle out of my medical bag and give it to him. I see he has four exposed bullets and two grazed his side. Now, do not move son, this is going to sting like hell."

I must have fallen asleep as they worked on me as they were gone when I woke up. It was hard to move or turn over without pulling the stitches in my back. The nurse came in when she heard me making a noise. She smiled even though she looked tired and probably sat outside all night.

I told her, "When I get out of bed to go to the bathroom, you climb in and get some sleep. I have things to do and someone to see."

"I beg your pardon; I am not getting into your bed with you."

I laughed and told her not to worry; I really do have a headache. That whiskey you gave me was rough. She insisted on changing the bandages and got into bed as I got out.

I asked her, "Aren't you going to get undressed before going to sleep?"

"Not until you leave."

I got washed and dressed before saying goodbye to her. In the bathroom I pulled out $3,000 to give to the defectors with a hole through the president's face. The couple was up and thanked me for the money as they has left everything behind in Czechoslovakia.

He pointed to the hole and said, "Is good."

I answered, "Yeah is good. It most likely came from your rifle."

"No not mine, my comrade who is no longer on earth, thanks to you putting a bullet in his head."

"He is in a better place now, thanks to me and if you were not in a hurry to defect you could be with him now. Let's go get something to eat."

Summerall was downstairs in his jeep as we came out of the barracks wanting to drive us to the mess hall. While we ate he mentioned that General Neuhofer came in during the night and wanted to drive me to Frankfurt. That was the last thing I wanted, to be in an Army sedan for four or five hours with Frank Neuhofer again. Why would he, since he is scheduled to be at the briefing next week.

When we arrived back at the ASA building, Neuhofer was there and ready to take the two guests with me to Frankfurt. We couldn't discuss anything in the car with them present. Of all the luck he had two sedans with two MPs, and we would be alone in the back seat of the trailing staff car with the defectors in the front car.

The drive was not that bad as we mainly talked about being back fishing in the Boca Grande Pass in a week. He did say that Kenny was going to pick me up and drive me straight to the hospital at Mildenhall Air Base about an hour and a half from London. This was just a routine checkup to dress my bandages. I thought to myself, *we will see if that is what is going to happen.*

After long drive I was dropped off on the curbside of the airport as he had to catch up with the two defectors and debrief them. When I arrived in London, Kenny was waiting in his usual parking place.

As I climbed in to his taxi he asked, "Where to Guv? Arrow or the Yank ospital."

"Harrow."

"Thought you say that. I was told you ad a bit of bother back over the wall. What was that all bout getting shot up. Them that did the shooting I bet didn't need no ospital, did they Guv."

I didn't say anything as he gazed into the rear view mirror hunched over his steering wheel. I let it go, but he couldn't.

"Thought so Guv, ere we are at number 24. . Shall I wait for you?"

"Yeah wait, I won't be long."

Kenny called me back to the taxi and told me, "I'll be taking you to the ospital guv, you're leaking oil, your back is wet."

Nicola came to the door and welcomed me home after three months away. I told her to be ready to travel to Florida in two days. I have to go to Mildenhall Air Base for them to change my bandages.

After she kissed me and I turned to go back to the taxi, she saw the blood and said, "I am going with you! Kenny, don't you dare leave without me. I will get my things."

We waited for her to join us. When she got into the taxi she was adamant on finding out why I had bloodstains on the back of my overcoat. The farther we drove the more boisterous she became as Kenny was eyeing us from the mirror.

He finally heard enough and said, "Your Yankee boy was shot and told im I did wot I was instructed to take im straight to the ospital, no ee wanted to see is gal first, ee did. Guv, I suggest you level wif er."

"Okay you two. After the doctor gets through with me then I will tell you everything that you need to know."

Kenny said, "That want wash Guv. The general told you in the past you ad to tell er everything. She deserves that much Guv."

I laughed and said, "You are sneaky, I'll give you that Kenny. You want to hear the gory details, do you?"

Kenny was chuckling up front and even more hunched over the steering wheel with looking back at me with a teasing twinkle in his eye.

"Okay, here is how it was. When I was crossing under the fence three Russian helicopters discovered me and tried to stop me from getting into the German side of the forest. They shot my motorbike and me. Saddlebags stopped the bullets from entering deeper into my back. Nothing else happened; it was a rather boring assignment."

"You need to get a normal job before we get married Billy, one that doesn't require you being shot at."

Kenny started in which wasn't going to help, "I reckon you ave been lucky so far Guv, with all the people you seemed to have made disappear and those that keep coming to find your where a bouts. I knew you weren't exactly kosher when we first met, if you don't mind me saying."

We pulled in front of the Air Force hospital just in time for these conversations to end, thank goodness.

We were met by emergency hospital workers and ushered into an operating room. The doctor in charge asked me to remove my clothes down to my trousers. He then ordered an orderly to take the clothes down to the laundry and have them back in an hour. He was ready to dress the bandages when he noticed the stitches needed re-stitching as they were pulled apart. A local anesthetic was administered this time and everything was taken care of.

Kenny then drove us to London just after an hour of being at the hospital. I was told by a medic to lie on the floor of the cab on my stomach and to get some sleep, and do not let anything touch my back.

When we arrived at the flat General Simpson was waiting for us inside. He was concerned that my going to Florida was not an intelligent move, and rescheduled the briefing for the next weekend in Brighton. So all of us were to stay at the Grand, Friday through Monday morning.

The general wanted to have another briefing in June on the Florida Island.

Nicola told the general that school didn't end until the beginning of July and could the trip be made then. Also, her mother and father would like to see where Billy grew up. That would be no problem according to Simpson, since the tarpon season would still be going strong.

The next morning Kenny was at the front door needing to talk to me. We walked down to the cafe by Hyde Park Corner and found a table in the corner that was away from other patrons. After ordering two full English breakfasts and getting stuck in to consuming it, Kenny got on with the information that needed to be reported as he pulled out his official undercover note book.

"First Guv, your ambassador as been seeing a new Russian. Now you did tell me to keep track of im didn't you Guv. They both even spent the odd night on the barge. The last time I took im there he didn't carry nothing and came out with a brown leather satchel. In the last three weeks they ave met at least four times. Something is up, I can feel it in me water if you catch me drift. Now the name e used on one occasion was Malik. E's a miserable so and so, never smiles or say's good morning or wot about da wefer."

"Thank you for the update Kenny. I have to get back and put the kettle on; Nicola will be waking up soon. Does the general owe you anything?"

"Right Guv, I'll stay for another cuppa. See if something comes up. I been paid even if I do nuttin, I still get an envelope anded to me every Friday."

# Chapter 11

## Briefings and Ambassador's Confrontation

It was still spring break for Nicola, affording us to shop and entertain our friends from Harrow and the team from Cambridge. Kenny reported the ambassador spent last weekend on the barge, and he drove him to Heathrow where Kenny was told to wait while the ambassador went to the Aeroflot ticket kiosk. That Friday Nicola and I wanted to be in Brighton by noon so we could have fish and chips on on the Pier.

We stayed away from the hotel lobby so we didn't run into the three generals or their wives and get bogged down into endless chatter. That evening a table was reserved and we could catch up on news then.

Nicola and I had to be in the lobby before the others as we were the unofficial host. We wanted to get a drink anyway, being early had its rewards. When most of the group joined us, we were ushered to our normal table in the back of the room.

We were waiting for Kenny when Simpson spotted the ambassador and his wife being swooned all over by the restaurant workers, even the chef came out in his oversize hat and white overcoat. The general grimaced with the ambassador approaching our table.

The ambassador said, "General Simpson, General Thibodeau, I wasn't told you two were having a get together; and who are these other two gentlemen and their lovely ladies?"

My back was to him as I stood up and introduced myself and the rest of the group.

I said, "We would like for you and your lovely wife to join us if it wasn't for us waiting on another couple. Are you here for the weekend, maybe you can join us tomorrow night for dinner, ambassador."

"Yes we are here until Sunday; however, we have a previous engagement. We are going to have dinner tonight overlooking the sea."

The ambassador and his wife left before Kenny showed up, thank God, that would have blown our whole eavesdropping organization. It wasn't like Kenny to be late; we were now worried about him. In the meantime, Simpson told us that the ambassador has been recalled and Richard Nixon has appointed someone very different, a person who will work with us and not against the agency.

General Simpson said, "The embassy has no one holding down the fort this weekend with his assistant in Washington D.C. For the next two weeks, I smell a rat. Wright, after our briefing tomorrow afternoon, how about taking a trip to see if anything is amiss around Grosvenor Square?"

"Yes sir. If you don't mind I will have Kenny drive me. Here he comes, I will ask him later."

Kenny said as he sat down, "Sorry ladies, gentlemen for me being late. The North Circular was choc a bloc for miles with accidents for the Friday coastal escape. No need to introduce the missus as you all know each other."

It was a nice evening with no one talking of covert actions or anyone being watched. After dinner, Nicola and I went dancing to a night club as the older folk went on to bed.

Thibodeau left a note under my door for me to meet him before taking off to London in the morning.

Nicola asked, "What is that all about, Billy?"

"Not sure. It is something he doesn't want the other two generals to know about. Once I meet him, Kenny will have the taxi out front of the hotel and I will not be able to come back to the room. Let's get some sleep; I have to be up in five hours."

The next morning it was imperative to get dressed and out without waking Nicola. General Thibodeau was waiting as I entered the breakfast room. He and Kenny seemed to be in a deep conversation when they noticed me with Kenny excusing himself to go get his taxi. I heard Kenny call the general Guv, which is a first; he said before that he didn't trust the general when he was the one in charge of the CIA at the embassy.

I asked General Thibodeau. "What was that all about? You seem to be giving my contact instructions."

"Don't get your knickers in a twist. What do you mean your contact, as I am signing for his wage packet every month he may belong to both of us. We will discuss who's man he is later."

"If you don't mind me asking General, isn't this a little clandestine with leaving the other generals out of our meeting this morning."

"Yes it is. The reason being is I do not want General Simpson to know what you have to do for me. It will be better for him if he is unaware, in case you get caught with your hands in the cookie jar. Kenny is out front, this won't take long. I have to tell you, first I think this is the ambassador's swan song; it is just a gut feeling. He is probably in Brighton to meet up with his KGB agent for last-minute instructions. We will discuss it this afternoon.

"Your number one goal Wright is to get into the ambassador's office and safe. The key to your office will open all of the doors on the top floor. This ambassador wanted it that way so he could have access to CIA files. His desk is the same as my old desk with the same secret drawer. He has a second safe like the one in the CIA chief;s office, look through the contents of both safes in his office. You know the combination I believe."

"No sir, I was never given the combination."

"Don't be coy with me. I've seen you study the numbers as I dialed them, the first chance you had to watch me open my safe. Anyway, I let you watch for a reason such as this assignment. Report back here to me at 1400 hours before the 1500 hour briefing. You better go. Oh, one more thing, you have been mentioned in earlier dispatches, so maybe they should be taken."

Kenny was waiting outside the cab and even opened the door for me, which is another first.

As he drove away I asked him."What is up with you? First, you said Guv to the general then you opened my door for the first time."

"Did I?"

That was all he said, so I played his little game and didn't comment anymore either all the way to London. All he did was chuckle a few times that exacerbated the situation even more.

"We are ere Guv. Be careful."

I departed the taxi as he stared in a school boy prank way. What did he mean by be careful?

The Marine MPs didn't notice or acknowledge me as I entered the elevator. The ambassador's door was accessible by the same key. I was astounded with the lack of security.

Nothing was found, both safes was cleaned out which was odd. I checked every inch of the office, even looked to see if anything was taped on the underside of his overpowering desk and each drawer. His residence had to be the most likely place or maybe they are packed for a trip.

I went back outside and instructed Kenny to drive up to the ambassador's residence. He almost knew this was the next stop.

As I opened the taxi door Kenny said, "It's under the small plant pot, Guv."

I laughed to myself thinking *that is where any thief would look*. This is going to go too fast; the key to the house was there under the smallest pot.

Once inside the alarm system was buzzing. I had maybe 45 seconds to find and disable the thing. It was in the cloak closet next to the door, another no, no, way too convenient.

I didn't have much time now so the most obvious place was his safe. He has a desk that matched the two large desks in the embassy. The safe was so easy to open an astute teenager could do it. It was full of cash in old American $100 bills. So much cash there was no room for files.

I loaded the cash into a linen clothes bag from the hotel. The desk was a treasure trove of telling documents and one Russian passport in the ambassador's name, and two American passports both in the ambassador and his wife's name.

Kenny blew his horn just as I stuffed everything into the same sack. I looked out and saw three MPs approaching the front door. I had to climb out a rear window and down a large cast iron drain pipe. I walked in the opposite direction of the waiting taxi and whistled. Kenny must have seen me standing in the middle of the street in his rear view mirror; he drove away and made a u-turn to pick me up.

When we drove away I asked Kenny to drive in front of the ambassador's residence again so I could see what the three MPs were up to. Two were standing guard on each side of the door and the other one must have gone inside to look around.

Kenny commented, "Close shave, Guv; I didn't see you come out the front."

"Yes it was a close shave. Those MPs were the biggest men I have ever seen and probably as mean as they are big. Now back to Brighton to see the general. On the way back you can tell me what you and Thibodeau were jawing over."

"Wots that legal word Guv, confidential, is it. I will tell you of one piece to your inquiring and really don't ave to, but since we go back awhile it is I am getting a pay raise. I guess I will now call him Guv, too, Guv."

Kenny must have thought his statement was clever or cute as he chuckled again. We didn't talk the rest of the way back, which was good as it gave me time to go through the ambassador's papers.

When I arrived the bellhop gave me a note from Thibodeau, asking I go straight to his room.

After knocking on the general's door and going inside, I emptied the bag on his bed and said, "I will be right back, Nicola doesn't know I am back."

"She is out shopping with the wives and will not be back until 5. How much cash do you think is there?"

"Each bundle contains $10,000 and there are 11 bundles. Look at the three passports and airline tickets."

"The ambassador has some explaining to do. One passport is missing and there is only one ticket to Moscow. The ticket receipt has two tickets paid for.

Oh my, this is a puzzle; you don't think he has fallen for the oldest trick in the book in falling in love with a Russian beauty."

"My assumption also, sir."

"Well done. I can't believe he left them inside the embassy. What a stupid thing to do."

"They were in his residence and no I did not break in as Kenny told me where the key was hidden. However, I had to breakout as three of the Marine's finest showed up as I was about to leave."

"You have 20 minutes to get ready for the briefing. I will see you on the pier at the furthermost bench."

"What about something to eat sir, I am starving."

"We will get fish and chips and have them as we talk; put on a heavy coat, the sea breeze is brazen."

We met at the fish bar with me as the lowest-ranking member was told to pay the man.

I was told by General Thibodeau, "The bench is barely long enough for us generals. You will stand in front and give the briefing on your last assignment only, the overseas action."

"Yes sir, but it is difficult to stand here in the cold wind, eat my fish and chips and give you the information; or am I supposed to block the wind so you three can eat? Besides, you already had lunch and I haven't."

Thibodeau said, "Quit your bellyaching and get on with it; we are getting cold waiting on you to fill us in on your last covert action. And while we are at it, where is the money that was left over? You know, the stuff that saved your life. You see we have read Summerall's report."

Since they already knew everything, I kept it short and as concise as possible with three generals feeding their faces and trying to squeeze ketchup out of small packets. They all had ketchup on their face. What a funny sight as I had to laugh.

General Neuhofer blurted out "What?" He wanted an explanation of why I was so rude.

"You guys have ketchup and grease all over your faces."

They looked at each other and started laughing. What a sight watching them wipe off the smudges on each other's faces. I was laughing so much it was impossible to finish my meal.

Simpson said, "What insolence, we will have you up on charges." At that moment I had a mouthful of chips and was trying to gulp them down.

Everyone was laughing so hard we had to throw the rest of the food away. We left the cold and found a secluded area inside the hotel bar to have a drink.

Thibodeau quietly said, "Wright that was the shortest briefing I have ever had attended. One thing is bothering us. The husband and wife you brought over the border may be a problem. What do you suppose we do with them?"

"I gave them $3,000 to start them on their new life. I suggest you take them to Langley soon, as they are still in a euphoric state. Train or brainwash them to be spies to work with or for me. I would bet within six months the wife will want to go home. Let her know the help I need is to get people out of the East and back inside when the need arises, and I will escort her back anytime."

General Simpson said, "They know you have killed and probably they know you as a ruthless thug."

"Yes sir. Tell them the help they give me will not require any violence. They will be able to come and go whenever they want, after I show them where to cross and how to avoid the authorities or soldiers."

Thibodeau asked, "Would you leave us now; we have to discuss your actions this morning."

"Yes sir. I will finish my beer upstairs while having a hot bath; my back is still numb sheltering you three from the wind. Get Nicola a double Scotch and soda when she walks in and tell her I am in the bath. Can one of you remember all of that?"

Thibodeau said, "You insolent SOB, Wright, giving three generals orders. We will see you drawn and quartered before the weekend is over."

The other two laughed out loud and as they said, *"Yeah, yeah."* They all three laughed and told me to get out, go have your bath.

A little later upstairs Nicola walked in and saw me in the bath with my bandages off. She noticed the wounds were healing, but still needed new bandages. She called the front desk for seven large bandages and rubbing alcohol. Back in the bathroom, she gave me a note from Tibby. I had to be in the bar one hour before we were to have dinner for one more meeting.

After telling Nicola duty calls and I will see her in an hour, I left for another briefing. This time it was on the documents found in the ambassador's residence. The three high-ranking intelligence officers were waiting for me with a pint of beer already pulled for me.

In a remote area of the lounge far away from the bar Thibodeau started the session with saying, "We have cataloged the cash and have perused the documents. The character in question is still in the hotel. We have decided to challenge him a day after tomorrow in the embassy, where he will be cornered and not able to escape. The copied dispatches with your name on them were not documented by us and were destroyed. As far as we know you are still anonymous here and in the Soviet Bloc countries, or at least your name is."

The ladies were now entering the lounge and Thibodeau said to me, "Would you take the ladies order and get them while we three senior officers entertain them."

While placing the drinks order at the bar, Kenny and his wife came up to ask the bar man something as I handed him the two drinks. The last three times

241

they were part of the group, they would always ask for the same drink.

We all settled on the plush leather couches and enjoyed the comradeship that had grown among us over the past 14 months.

Kenny raised his glass and said, "To the lovely ladies."

The rest of the evening was delightful as Kenny was in his element keeping everyone's attention with tales of war stories and how the Brits weathered the bombings, and how through dark times new friendships blossomed. The only time the three generals talked business was when they followed me to the loo. In the bathroom they told me they were going to bed soon and I should do the same. They have arranged to have the kitchen staff open the breakfast room up three hours. I was told to be down for a meeting at 0500 sharp.

The next morning they were ready as I was ushered into a back conference room. Breakfast, tea and coffee was on its way. Each of them had legal pads and folders for taking notes. I was told to keep everything in my head as I didn't need to have any notes left in my residence.

First thing that was discussed was what to do with the ambassador's money. One of the three thought it would be a good idea to buy the London property overlooking Hyde Park. I couldn't agree fast enough and added if any money was leftover just maybe buy some new kitchen appliances.

They all looked at me as if I had lost my mind, using agency swag to fit a new kitchen. This brought much laughter and stopped me from making any other suggestions. They hashed it over and came up with the answer. A new kitchen it was going to be, so they could entertain when I was away; and their wives would be happy to spend more time in the area.

The only thing wrong now with this scenario is I would have to be kept busy behind the Iron Curtain to also be out of the area. I was also asked what were my plans for the next two months as a tutor was set up to teach me how to speak Russian. The tutor was contracted to be in my place five days a week to prepare me for an assignment. This job was to be formulated in Langley with help from ASA headquarters in Frankfurt and Bad Aibling. I just listened to all of this chatter without being asked anything for now or if I wanted another mission.

One didn't have to be a brain surgeon to know the next assignment would be in Mother Russia itself. Most likely it is still on the drawing board with targets and assets penciled in. It couldn't be soon as there was some unfinished business with the ambassador, and what to do about him or with him. Anyway, this was for now just chitchat with a lot of hyperbole thrown in.

# Chapter 12

## The Reluctant Double, Double Agent

General Thibodeau started the official meeting off saying, "Wright, we have talked over what must be done about the ambassador. We will arrest him as he and his Russian girlfriend enter Heathrow, and then fly them both to Washington on Thibodeau's plane. They both will be incarcerated at the Fort Leavenworth Prison."

I interrupted by telling and asking them, "If you do that I have to get into the residence and place the Russian passport back in the safe. I would like to ask you three wise men: How many agents do we have that are KGB informants or plants?"

Thibodeau was in command as he was the only one saying something informative. The other two were contributing by saying, here, here, we agree.

"We have tried many times to get someone close to the Russian secret service and failed each time. We had to go cap in hand to retrieve these agents and trade valuable assets for them. It seems you have something in mind, please enlighten us."

"We can turn Ambassador Wilfred and his wife into agents. Ambassador Stevens is broke and his wife, a Boston blue blood, feeds on being an ambassador's wife. She loves having servants to wait on her and her upper crust friends. The embarrassment of having her husband incarcerated and the publicity from being taken in by a prostitute will follow her to the grave, not to mention also back to Boston. He should to be appointed ambassador to Moscow."

I paused, waiting for a response with none coming I started again by saying, "Give me two days and if they aren't on board, we or you can hang them out to dry. Lastly I will take over his Russian alias as the KGB Colonel Victktor Rastoff and watch the Stevens while in Moscow. The American ambassador in Moscow is being recalled next month anyway, so the Russians will be none the wiser."

The three of them talked among themselves for a few minutes and General Simpson said, "If this works, you will not only be a colonel in the Russian KGB, you will be promoted to colonel in the U.S. Army next year."

"Thank you, sir. When you see the ambassador, ask if you could set up a meeting at their residence tomorrow at noon. I will take your place and report back to you in the afternoon at the London flat; or if you want to get away sooner, General Simpson can call you on the outcome."

We finished the meeting as the ladies and Kenny came into the room to get us. They all were taken aback when they learned we have been at it for four hours. The ambassador walked up to the front desk as Simpson excused himself to make the appointment.

When he came back he whispered in my ear, "That arrogant oaf wants to have the meeting at 10 a.m. instead of noon. I wanted to frog march that SOB right then and there out of the lobby. Get that scoundrel good and give me the sordid details tomorrow. I will have the MPs stand by if the Stevens become awkward and refuse your offer."

Nicola asked, "What is going on darling? Is anything wrong?"

"Do you mind if we leave today and spend the tonight in the flat? We can go to Flanigan's for supper and then to Soho night clubbing."

"Oh darling that would be absolutely marvelous. You do come up with so many groovy things to do."

Thibodeau muttered, "I bet he does."

"What did he say darling, I didn't understand one word; he seemed to mumble."

"He said he wished he were as young and handsome as I am."

General Simpson blushed as the rest of us laughed, and he then seemed to be amused or acted like it.

We all departed as Kenny drove Thibodeau, Neuhofer and their wives to the airport. We went to London by train and Simpson and his wife stayed another night in Brighton, so he could be away while the ambassador and his wife were being coerced into working for the CIA network in Moscow.

The next morning Nicola traveled back to Harrow to start the new school semester as Kenny came through the door wanting to go for a big English fry up at his cafe across from the KGB safe house.

In the cafe we were sitting at a side counter watching the Russian flat when the ambassador's girlfriend went in. She never came out again by the time we left to go to the ambassador's residence. Kenny was curious how I became close enough to be invited to the boss' house. I told him something like, "I was summoned for being a bad boy and needed a telling off. No need to go any further on this conversation." When Kenny dropped me off he said he would wait down the street.

I rang the door bell at precisely 10 a.m. The butler opened the door and looked at me as if I was a tramp wanting a hand out, with his thin nose pointed towards the sky.

I sarcastically said, "General Simpson couldn't make it, so he sent me to meet the Stevens. Is that okay with you?"

He showed me into the drawing room where they both were waiting. The butler showing his displeasure cleared his throat in a way that conveyed his displeasure with me being in the house.

I said to the butler, "You must have your throat looked into, it could be contagious."

The ambassador spoke loudly, "Now see here, whoever you are. Get out. Winston, show this person to the door."

"Before I go, can I ask if you have seen Colonel Rastoff recently or have you looked into a mirror lately?"

The ambassador turned beet root, as the Cockneys would say. He asked the butler to leave the room. When the butler left I could still feel Winston's presence, eavesdropping at the door as he wanted to listen in to what I was doing there.

I opened the door quickly making him fall against my chest.

I pushed him outside and whispered, "You try another stunt like that and you will need your balls sewn back on."

Stevens said, "This is prosperous, I will have the MPs escort you out of my home and thrown in jail. How do you know about Rastoff?"

"Later on Stevens, now before you have me arrested have a look in your wall safe and your desk safe."

While he was gone I told his wife, "You are going to hear some unpleasant things said about your husband this morning. Whatever you do, think before you talk. I promise, you will come out of this situation wearing the pants in this house."

She looked at me as if I were stark raving mad. The ambassador came into the room and put his small weak hands around my neck trying to choke me. I stood up and pushed him away as I turned around.

He said, "You crook, where is my money?"

His wife entered the confrontation asking, "What money? We do not have any money."

He told her, "Shut your stupid mouth, you have nothing to say in this house outside of the bedroom."

He just lit the fuse as I motioned to her to stay calm with the palms of both hands pointing down. She acknowledged my wishes with her hands placed on her knees.

The ambassador demanded, "I want the money and my papers or I will shoot you myself; do you understand how much trouble you are in?"

"Wilfred, I would suggest you sit down and listen for once in your life."

"You are not permitted to call me by my first name; it is Mr. Ambassador to you or Mr. Stevens if you wish."

Mrs. Stevens asked her husband and me again, "What money?"

I then told her, "Angie, your husband had over $100,00 in his safe from selling secrets to the Russians. He had a passport in the name of Colonel Victktor Rastoff with his photograph in the document."

"You're a liar. Don't believe anything he says. Leave us Angie."

She answered him in a forceful tone, "No damn you, I have a right to know everything."

"Sit down ambassador and let me explain what we are prepared to do to help you out of this mess you are in."

He rang the Marine MP call button. Two MPs were in the room within two minutes and grabbed the ambassador by his arms to escort him to a secure room in the embassy. I ordered them to wait outside the door and make sure the butler did not come anywhere close to this room as he is under suspicion as well.

Ambassador Stevens then sat down and listened as I told his wife about the prostitute he was leaving with tomorrow, and the documents he was going to give to the KGB on his arrival in Moscow.

"This is what you are going to do Wilfred, or you will be going to Leavenworth for the rest of your life. Mrs. Stevens please leave the room and wait for me in upstairs in your bedroom."

After a few minutes to allow Mrs. Stevens to leave the room I continued, "Alright Stevens, you are going to work for the CIA as a double agent in Moscow under the cover of being the ambassador or spend the rest of your life in a cage," I told him sternly.

"Do you understand ambassador that you will be required to pass on to your pals' information you are given. You will gather names of Russian agents working in Europe and the Americas. . I will personally keep an eye on you as you perform your new duties. Your girlfriend is now on her way to a federal women's prison for espionage crimes against the United States. Your wife is waiting for me. Stay here until I get back and have your reply ready. The MPs will take you away if you leave this room."

The two MPs were ordered to go into the drawing room to keep the ambassador from leaving or making any phone calls. The butler was told to leave the premises and his things would be on the front doorstep tomorrow morning.

Upstairs, I met with Mrs. Stevens into her bedroom and closed the door so we could get on with the main part of the plan.

I was strict with her saying, "Your husband is facing a life sentence in federal prison. You are broke and have nothing to go back to in Boston, except a waitress job at some breakfast bar. I am offering you a way out, Angie, if you agree to my terms. Wilfred will be given the ambassadorship in Moscow and you can continue to impress your Boston friends. If you go back to Boston as the wife of a traitor and penniless you will be shunned, as you well know."

"What do you want of me? How can I help?"

"I want you to keep an eye on Wilfred and make sure he never strays off the reservation again. I will need an escort whenever I am in Moscow and you will be my escort. I want to meet you tomorrow afternoon at Kings Cross Station at noon for lunch; don't be late, you are working for me as of today. You will be getting a wage when you get to Moscow, money to be paid to you in cash. Do not let Wilfred know about our arrangement and I will guide you on what is expected of you."

"That would make me happy to get even with that two-timing charlatan."

Angie got up from sitting on the bed to give me hug and then kissed me as her way of saying thank you for letting her continue being the ambassador's wife.

I left the house taking the two Marines with me to stand guard outside and not to let anyone in or out except me or General Simpson for the next seven days. Two Marine MPs were to stand guard at the back of the residence.

The general was in his office and was excited that the ambassador had his bottom spanked. I went over all of the details including my suspicions of the butler being a KGB plant. The butler's personal items should be gone through to see if he was a spy.

He excused me so I could get back to the apartment and run up to Cambridge for a meeting with the team and a report on the professor.

After staying the night in Cambridge to find the ops center was working, I returned to London the next morning and hurried to meet Angie for lunch.

Angie was on time and as we sat down in the transport cafe she looked different. She was attractive, being a little older made her look sophisticated, in a sexy way. Her dress was shorter and tighter, not quite a minidress but close to it. Her dark eyes and hair made her look a little like Elizabeth Taylor now instead of a downtrodden wife.

I asked her, "Tell me everything your husband said when I left and do you trust him not to report me any officials from this day forward?"

"He kept quiet most of the day, to himself. No, he is not to be trusted ever again. I am sure he is trying to work out how to get this behind him and destroy whoever caused this situation. You undoubtedly will have a target on your back."

"Look, Angie, you have to get over this jilted wife stuff and clear your senses of the enmity you feel towards him. He cannot hurt me as much as I can affect the rest of his life. This is business between me and you, no one else. I really do not care how much you feel cheated on or out of. Let's start over again, what happened yesterday afternoon and last night?"

"Yesterday he never went to his office and he canceled all of his appointments. He apologized and cried all day for me to forgive him. Last night I put his clothes out in the hall and told him to find another bed to sleep in. That was all that happened yesterday; this morning we didn't say a word at the breakfast table."

I thought to myself that this is going to be the worst environment for my new agent to be in. I had to do something now before the hatred destroyed her and rendered her useless in keeping an eye on him.

It was imperative for me to win her over so a bond could be formed, while she was still feeling alone and hurt. Nicola was always in the back of my mind as more of a conscience angel to keep my work as business and not personal. After we finished with lunch I took her to my flat and seduced her, which was quite effortless as she probably wanted to get even with her husband.

After our close association I then gave her 500 pounds for her first six months wages. It was unreported Russian money anyway, and didn't come out of the firm's bank account. It was important to start training her now on how to act around her husband.

After telling her she had to move back into the bed with her husband she was shocked and said, "You are a cold bastard."

"Angie, you are going to have to think differently or more likely departmentalize the way you live. From this day on, you will look after yourself and me in a way that will keep both of us alive when we are in Moscow and a functioning team. I want to see you tomorrow again over lunch. This time we will meet at the pub inside Victoria Station at the same time as today."

"Wright, you really think someone would kill us if they knew we were working together. Who would do such a thing?"

"The Russians would in a heartbeat and they would have your husband back in their clutches."

We parted as almost lovers and not adversaries. It could have turned nasty if she thought I was just using her to spy on her husband and with no chance of her getting some support from me. During the last year I have learned one valuable lesson, besides money, emotions can be used for seeking loyalty.

General Thibodeau was waiting downstairs in Kenny's taxi as Mrs. Stevens left to go home. He got out when she was out of sight.

Thibodeau asked, "What in the blazes was she doing coming out of the flat? This does not look good Will."

"She has to get her mind right, she has to get past the emotional upheaval of her two-timing husband. Don't worry, sir."

"I won't worry; you seem to have a sixth sense on getting people on board. The other two directors have another assignment in mind for the end of the year. In the meantime keep studying the Russian language. We will discuss it towards the end of June on Gasparilla Island."

"I have my first tutorial tomorrow for seven hours and will be involved in that over the next two months. General, you have to have the couple from Czechoslovakia ready and trained by then."

The general left and I went out to purchase notepads and a large blackboard on wheels. The next morning my tutor arrived at 8 a.m. and we got started right away. The Russian lady looked like Brumhilda from some German gulag. She was thorough and wasn't fond of any joking around. I sent her off to have lunch at 11:30 and told her to be back at 1:30.

Angie was on time and wasted no time in giving me a kiss, and she held my hand as we walked into the pub as if we were deeply in love. She reported that her husband was a different person this morning after she let him move back into her bedroom. I told her that she seemed to be a little different also. We set up our next meeting at the same time the following Monday, and then she was off to the States before joining her husband in Moscow in three weeks.

When I got back to the flat Brumhilda was waiting outside with a disgruntled look on her face. I had a feeling our afternoon session was going to be a torturous one.

This tutoring went on for a long time that day and many weeks that followed. During this time I kept all of my appointments centered around the lunch hour, and not making the big lady wait outside again for me to return from some pub lunch.

It was the middle of June, Brumhilda was satisfied I had progressed enough and could speak Russian fluently. She had a way of making me learn as I wanted to be rid of her ASAP.

Nicola and I left for Florida the last day of June to meet up with the generals and their wives. Boca Grande was really hot and humid when we got there in that first evening.

# Chapter 13

## The Russian Connection

Nicola and I arrived on Gasparilla Island two days before the generals were to arrive. Our main task was to get their rooms ready and have workbooks for the briefing, or that was my thought. We were planning on three days of meetings with fishing for tarpon in the afternoon. The next day we traveled to the Wright farm in Eastern Hillsborough County between Riverview and Brandon. There are two sleepy little farming towns with one grocery store between them.

At mom's after Sunday lunch, the boys played a pickup game of touch football while the sisters and family got to know a little about Nicola. In the late afternoon we left to travel the three-hour trip back before it got too late, and would miss the sun going down over the Gulf of Mexico.

That evening the three generals and their wives arrived tired and jet lagged. They went straight to bed and we wouldn't see them until breakfast was served. I woke up at 4 a.m. by someone talking downstairs. The three wise men were wide awake and ready to get the briefing started.

I went back and got the lined workbooks with General Thibodeau saying, "Take those books back upstairs; this briefing isn't taking place, at least on paper."

After getting back downstairs again, the three men were out on the front deck with four large rocking chairs placed in a circle.

Thibodeau started the first session with saying, "Wright, we have gone over what is required of you the rest of the year. You will travel to Moscow under the alias of Colonel Rastoff to find a suitable apartment to use within two weeks. Your ticket on Aeroflot is waiting for you at the ticket counter at Heathrow Airport. I would assume you have Mrs. Stevens under your control by now and her husband is behaving himself. The two defectors are progressing through the farm with flying colors and will be ready to relocate to Moscow in December."

"I do not have to tell you again that if you get caught impersonating a Russian colonel you will be shot. The chances are we will assume you are dead if your dispatches cease to continue."

General Neuhofer added his instructions, "Take the next two months to practice your Russian language skills. In October, you are scheduled to meet up with the ASA team again to take the two defectors back into Czech territory for a training run. You will have to enter through Bratislava as the Czech border fence will be fully reinforced by that time.

"The two defectors will be delivered back to the farm after crossing back into West Germany for their last month of training. Are there any questions Wright?" General Neuhofer asked.

"Good, I didn't think so. Let's go catch a tarpon, the charter captain is waiting at the dock."

The next two days were a repeat of the first briefing until it was drummed into me. The generals left to go home, while Nicola and I stayed the last week relaxing. One of the wives let it slip out that I was going to Moscow on a covert assignment. I had to assure Nicola it was just a plan and nothing was certain.

We arrived back in Britain with Nicola being dropped off in Harrow and me telling her I was on a job for the next two months. She didn't take that well as she asked is the Russian trip past the planning stage. We were both jet lagged since we talked all the way across the Atlantic and needed to get some sleep.

The next day I went to have Sunday lunch in Harrow. After having roast lamb and stuffing with lots of veggies, Nicola and I cleared the table and washed up. During the washing up I told her that I would be leaving in the morning and may not be back for a while. It was mainly because the trip may run into another assignment. However, I would have some of July and August off. She wasn't so upset at that since she would be spending most of the summer alone.

The next day when I got to Moscow, Angie was waiting as I went through Russian security. She told me that Wilfred was being so good it was a shame that she still wanted to be with me instead. She also wanted me to know that she found a nice apartment overlooking Red Square that would be perfect for us.

We went straight to the flat with the taxi driver being so much like a typical KGB agent, he didn't have to advertise the fact he was one. No one followed us, which is suspect when a Russian officer comes home, especially from the West.

The flat she picked was way too small and offered no real vantage point to seeing the Kremlin. That night I had to stay in the Moscow Intercontinental and found the flat I needed the next day. It had to have two bedrooms with a view, a garage, and be on the second floor backing onto an alley.

Angie and I were inseparable for the next two weeks as I trained her on what to look for and how to study ordinary people. She was a quick learner and became an astute judge of character as we studied commuters in the main train station for hours. We traveled all over the place with her on the back of the motorcycle she bought for me; we drove across Red Square as a silly thing to do. I left Angie to go back to London with instructions for her to entertain and befriend as many as possible KGB and Kremlin officials.

August and September went by way too fast as I had to go back to work, and Nicola back to teaching elementary school. The two people I brought out of the Czech Republic months ago were arriving in Frankfurt on Friday. I had to meet them with General Neuhofer's driver taking us to Bad Aibling. I thought of many scenarios on how the two defectors should be trained. First, I had to know what their names were; this small detail was lost in every dispatch for good reason.

It was Friday morning and catching the 7 a.m. BEA flight was going to get me to Frankfurt at 9 with the one-hour time difference. Clearing customs was going to be a little faster than their Trans Atlantic flight and we all should be through about the same time.

After waiting for them to come through immigration, we had a brief meeting and went outside. The driver was waiting as we walked into the cool October air. All the way to Bad Aibling we talked and I learned their names again, Alex and Isla Gustoff. They were excited about going back home to see their friends again, and were also satisfied living in the West. They knew that once the last month of their training was over, they had to relocate to Moscow for at least a year.

We planned to go over and get them to Isla's hometown where I would leave them for one week and meet up again in the Hotel Jalta in Prague. We would work out of the hotel for three days and then return to Bratislava to cross back over to West Germany.

Summerall was waiting on the front steps as we pulled up to his headquarters. He took us to the mess hall along with the team before introductions were exchanged. As we walked I slowed the first sergeant down to ask him a question.

I wanted to know if he received my message about bugging the Gustoff"'s room. He assured me it was well compromised by three listening devices, and one was so obvious I could go in with them to disconnect it to show them good faith.

We all went back to the ASA office after a late lunch to begin the logistics on the action in two days. There were aerial photographs of the border and where we thought was the best place to cross over. I would go over a day before the two guests to arrange transportation and meet them back at the fence.

We talked over our strategy for four hours without a break and left to have supper. We all had to go together for obvious security reasons with the old man signing again for the food. We then left for the barracks to show the guests their room. Everyone waited outside while I went in to see if the accommodations were adequate for our guests. When we went in, I closed the door behind us and looked around. I asked Alex to look for any listening devices like he was trained to do at the Langley farm. I let him find the obvious one on top of a bedside lamp. I took the device and put it in my pocket, and asked them to see if another one was present.

Alex found one in the bathroom behind the toilet. I said, "Great, you have passed your first test. Good night, I will be here at 7 a.m. to take you to breakfast, now get some sleep. Tomorrow is going to be another long day."

The old man and I went with the team to listen in on the two to see what they were all about. The first sergeant was already listening in and said we were being tested by those two. Alex whispered in Russian, which was strange since Isla was supposed to be Czech; and he next said in English, "Let's look around the base in the morning before we meet with the Yanks."

The first sergeant suggested that these two were not what they seem. Tomorrow they will be given old classified information to see if they discuss them tomorrow night in the bedroom. I suggested that we think about the content as they would have gone over old classified stuff on the farm as a training guide.

I suggested that we use something more up-to-date like the new Russian town that is being constructed. The couple went to sleep and we decided that we all should do the same.

The rest of us left to get some sleep. I woke up early, but couldn't let on I was awake in case they twigged that they were listened to. It was 5 a.m. when they walked downstairs and outside. I didn't dare open the curtains as that would have been the clue they needed.

The two defectors looked around outside for about two hours, which was not good. One could only imagine the reasons they really wanted to look around. There was really nothing outside to photograph or explore, only classified files inside the ASA office.

# Chapter 14

## Trapping the Mole

The Gustoff's after returning to their room, came down as they pretended to have just woken up. The two were taken over to the mess hall by Summerall, with the rest of the team walking quickly together to catch up. The first sergeant tugged at my shirt to get me to slow down as he wanted to say something.

The first sergeant said, "Wright, we have a problem that will not be resolved by being nice. From what was heard the man is a mole and his wife is a reluctant participant. We will discuss this later when the team is alone."

The couple was dropped off at the barracks after leaving the mess hall, and asked to be ready in an hour to go over the schedule. Back at headquarters the team was assembled to discuss what was heard while the first sergeant listened in to Mr. and Mrs. Gustoff's conversation early this morning.

The first sergeant was asked to proceed as he started to go over his notes.

He said, "There were some damning aspersions by the man on Americans. The wife was not allowed to voice an opposite opinion and when she tried she was abruptly told to keep quiet in Russian. Somehow he got a message to the Russians on the location and time of the crossing. We believe they managed to get off the base and had help in making a phone call. We need to scrap the assignment; however, I think the woman can be an asset in setting up the Moscow network. It is up to you Wright on going on or scrapping it altogether."

"Thank you sergeant, first we have to get a code to General Thibodeau and Neuhofer to tell them the garden has moles and how should we deal with them. I will need help in dealing with Mr. Gustoff in the way of having a fake American passport with his photograph and the name of William Wright. Just maybe we can be rid of him and convince the Russians they have Billy in custody. We need to go to the woods a day later and have him leave the compound again in the morning to make another call on the change of plans, and see what phone he is using," I explained.

"Someone needs to take one of the Russian Luger's and fit six blanks in the chamber to be part of a cunning plan. We need to pretend that there is only one gun, and have it handed to me when we are on the bus loaded with blanks. Act surprised when I tell one of you to give it to Alex to carry for me, as I will be caring a satchel with money in it. We need to act as if those two are part of the team.

"There is a need to deflect any concerns they may have by going outside and throwing a football around, so they think we are relaxed and are taking life lightly. I will throw the football to Alex in a way he can easily catch it. The first sergeant needs to clap his hands and tell him good catch. Let's all go outside now and wait for them."

The two were picked up by the old man, and when they arrived the football plan worked. Alex threw it to me, and I ran past Isla handing her the ball very gently and told her to follow me so no one could touch her. She enjoyed the game with Alex fuming when she became the center of attention.

It was time to start the briefing when Alex put a damper on the game saying we were all being childish. The plan worked better than expected. In the conference room the two gave their passports to Summerall; he left to photograph their pictures and instructed the company clerk to get them published and take them to the forger. He handed the passports back as quickly as possible so as not to cause any suspicion.

At the end of the briefing Summerall congratulated me on my last mission in discovering the new Russian city being built. As I stood up everyone clapped when I was handed a document of a job well done. Alex was the only one who wasn't pleased. He had no idea it was a blank diploma with a ribbon. The old man mentioned that the action was being delayed one day because thunderstorms were forecast for tomorrow night.

Alex protested and said, "The schedule must be kept, and you would have time if no one played anymore games like children."

We ignored him and broke for lunch with everyone going overboard telling our guest how the old man managed to get the best chef in the Army to come here. That was not popular either with Alex. He must really miss Mother Russia by now as his lack of anything foreign was showing through.

The first sergeant who towered over Alex, slapped him on the back as he said to him, "Let's get some chow, Alex, that will make you feel better."

Again Isla was thrilled with the comradeship being shown to them while Alex acted like a spoiled teenager. On the way over Summerall told me to drive Isla to his house, so his wife could take her shopping for a suitable overcoat she will need on the crossing. Alex was not happy losing sight of his partner and protested the arrangement.

When I drove Isla to what she thought was the Summerall house and no one answered the door, we decided to go shopping anyway.

We shopped for several hours and became as close as anyone could in such a short time. She wanted a coat that was trendy with black faux patent leather that may be okay on a London street, but not suitable for hiking through the forest. We both laughed and bought it anyway. She grabbed my hand as we walked in the village, she said she was having the best time in a long time. We went into a cafe to have a drink; this is when she opened up about who she was and did not want to go back with us tomorrow.

I told her, "You do not have to go, tell Alex you have to go see a doctor."

"Alex will not let me stay no matter how sick I seem to be. You must not go Billy. Alex is not your friend. You are so nice, I fear for your safety."

I thanked her for caring what happens to me and bent over the table and kissed her for quite a long time. She moved to a chair next to me, as she wanted another kiss.

She then admitted, "Alex is not what he seems, please stay with me for one more day and we could run from him."

"Does Alex know who I am?"

"Yes, he suspects you are the one that has done so much damage to friends of the Soviet Union. You are the reason he was dropped on that fateful day and was allowed to come get me. It was all a set up, as you Americans say. He is an angry person and very strong physically to go with strong hate."

"How long have you been married and were you married in Russia?"

"No Billy, we are not married. We were paired up in class as were others to act out being married."

"Isla would you work with me in the future if it can be arranged that you become a paid adviser and coworker? However, you could get a normal job."

"There are friends in Russia I would like to help get free if it is possible. Yes, working with you for pay is good, too."

"Isla, we have to get back, the meeting will be over soon."

We both climbed in the jeep with Isla putting her hands on the back of my neck and giving me a very seductive kiss before starting the engine. She wanted to go park somewhere so we could do more than kiss. I thought that she may still be an operative, a good actor that made this all seem too good to be true. This is not the time for being vane. I thought that she was on the level and needed someone in her life. Still, I'd rather be unsure than careless.

When we arrived back at headquarters Alex started to give Isla the rough treatment. I started his way. Summerall stepped in and ordered me into his office. He slammed the door and loudly excoriated me so the visitors could hear a good old-fashioned ass chewing.

While this was going on the first sergeant took everyone to get dinner and to be out of the way.

When everyone was gone Summerall asked, "Did it work?"

"Like it was scripted in Hollywood."

"What did my wife say when you were at the door."

"I knocked on another door where it looked like no one was home."

"Good, okay Wright, we will go to the mess hall, when the group comes back for you to avoid Alex. Then you get some sleep. You will have to set your alarm for 3 a.m. and go see where he makes his calls. I want the person helping him here in this town. It grieves me a foreign spy is working on our turf."

I did as was ordered and was able to get seven hours sleep with waking up in time to shut off the clock alarm. After getting dressed, I climbed out the window and made my way to the front gate.

The first sergeant found where the wire was cut from our defector earlier in the day. I used the same route as he and waited on the edge of the village. It wasn't long before he showed up and met a man no more than 20 yards from me. They talked for a few minutes and Alex left to go back to the base.

The man in a sloppy well-worn brown suit with no tie waited, and then eventually walked in the opposite direction. He was watching to see if anyone was trailing Alex. Down a narrow cobblestone alleyway, he entered a small hotel as a light was turned on in a second floor bedroom. That was when I turned to go back to the base. I couldn't climb up to my room, so I went to see if the first sergeant was listening in to the conversations.

The sergeant poured me a cup of coffee and said, "That wife of his was knocking on your door and calling your name before he was barely out of the building. I don't believe it, how do you do it? How is that pretty little thing at the hotel? Is her name, Linda?"

"Lenka. We are friends and nothing more."

"Good night Wright, I am going into the conference room while you listen in. Ha ha, just friends my butt."

He was still laughing as he closed the door behind him. Alex was giving Isla a hard time about yesterday and threatened to have her re-trained when they got back to Moscow.

Summerall was early enough to catch the first shirt sleeping. He laughed at the big guy with a green wool Army blanket that looked like it should be covering a child. I told him about this morning and where he could find the go between.

He woke the sergeant up and said to him, "Let's go, we got a mole in the garden."

I went to my office to get a pistol for protection without the other two knowing about it. When we got to the hotel, Summerall ordered the sergeant to stay with the clerk while we went to the foreign agent's room. We were given a key and opened it ever so slowly and just as quietly. The man was sleeping soundly with an empty vodka bottle on the nightstand.

Before waking him I looked for a gun in the drawer and found nothing. I motioned to Summerall that the gun is in his bed. Summerall slapped him and when he bolted up the gun came out of the covers and in his hand. He almost got to the point of having it pointed at Summerall as I had my gun behind me and was able to shoot his hand.

When he dropped the gun I pointed my weapon at the man's head and said in Russian, "Say goodbye, this is your last day on earth."

The man soiled his bed at that precise moment with Summerall saying, "No Wright, we need him. Christ Almighty, you are crazy."

I said in Russian, "Brady, he's not going to tell you anything. I can't afford to have him walk out of here."

I lowered the gun once more towards his head and put it in his opened mouth.

He jerked back and told Summerall in Russian, "I will talk, I will talk."

Summerall said in Russian to me, "Get the hell out of here you maniac, and get the sergeant up here."

The sergeant hurried upstairs as I watched the clerk. He talked like a canary when he saw my pistol sticking out of the jacket. He knew the man was a foreign agent and from now on he would call our office when someone suspicious checked in.

I told him in German, "Sorry, we can't take the chance you not telling on us again. We will get our own man in here. Now run for it while I count to three."

The first sergeant came down with the Russian to see the hotel owner crying like a baby.

The captain said, "What is this all about?"

"He would also like to confess to his misbehaving, sir."

"What do you suggest I do with these two now?"

"There are a lot of empty cells not being used in Nuremberg right now."

Eventually, two MPs showed up to take the two scoundrels away in different vehicles.

On the way back to the base Summerall said, "I didn't authorize you to go armed, Wright."

"Sir, I never go into a hostile situation without protection."

The first sergeant and the old man were shaking their heads so much I said, "I am worried boys that your heads are going to fall off with all that shaking."

Brady Summerall said, "Pull behind the base sergeant and let's beat this smart ass to one inch of his life for putting our lives in jeopardy."

"Yes sir, how many times have we wanted to do just that in the last two years, sir?"

They started to laugh as we pulled up to the office. The buck sergeant asked the first shirt how it went with him replying, "You don't want to know, Buck."

Our guests were still in their rooms as I borrowed a stepladder to crawl into my bedroom to open the door. I then walked into the hall and saw Isla come out of her room. We walked downstairs while Alex was getting dressed. At the bottom of the stairs, she hugged me as we kissed for what seemed forever. I was afraid Alex was going to see us. She admitted to knocking on my door and it was lucky I didn't answer as Alex came back too soon.

I told her I would see her later, I had something to do. She had to have felt my gun, but said nothing. I took the ladder back and joined the team in going over this morning's activity. They all stared at me when I entered the building.

I hesitated as they looked at me and then I said, "What?"

They all looked funny, shaking their heads in unison with each other.

Summerall and the first shirt both commented that I was never allowed to go on any more assignments with them. I was on my own and God help me if I needed backup because it would not be forthcoming. We all had a good laugh at those ridiculous comments.

Summerall said, "Seriously, Wright, what are you going to do about going over the border with those two? You are being set up."

"I know. The woman will be so sick she will need a doctor when we leave tomorrow. We have to convince him to abort the mission, and he will probably want to go without her since he has already called in a different plan into his superiors twice in the last two days. I will stay quiet unless something needs to be said to upset him," I replied.

"I know he wants to hand me over to the KGB since he is assuming I am Billy, the covert agent. They are walking this way, let's go to the back of the property and throw the football around."

The two guests were directed to the back of the building to witness us playing with the football. Alex called us all over to see if we are ready to get on with the briefing, since no one suggested breakfast instead of playing like children. The team was now really up to their eyes with this jerk's snide comments. He was easier to goad into a reaction than a 3 year old.

We were now committed to starting the assignment tomorrow after daybreak with going to a new crossing point. I would go over first as a scout and make sure the path was clear to cross and return to escort the jerk. For the rest of the day, we packed our gear and studied the aerial photographs of the border area where West Germany, Bratislava and Czechoslovakia met.

That night a special meal was prepared for the team. It was to be oysters on the half shell, marinated Chateaubriand, with a chocolate éclair covered with vanilla ice cream. I asked the old man to have the chef prepare the plates before we get there. We all were to have half dozen oysters each with Isla having to try just one. The one for her was to be left out in room temperature for two hours before we arrive. That evening the dinner was served with German white wine with the starters and four bottles of Chateauneuf Du Pape served with the steaks.

The next morning we all gathered at the barracks to set off for the woods with box lunches stacked in the bus for three meals each.

Alex came downstairs to say Isla was up half the night with stomach cramps, diarrhea and throwing up from food poisoning. She needs a doctor soon.

I got off the bus and told the old man, "We have to scrap this exercise and wait a few days to wait for Isla to recover."

Alex became boisterous and demanded we leave her behind. It was settled, we took off on the bus with the first sergeant going over again what was expected of us all. I was called on to go over what I was going to do on the scouting trip.

I started with saying, "I will be the first to go across to make sure the pathway is clear of soldiers, and to find a vehicle in which we can travel to Prague in."

Gustoff interrupted and said, "This is idiotic planning. We will go together and do the scouting, and not waste any time coming and going. I will be in charge; I know the area better than anyone."

Summerall said, "If that is the way he wants it, fine; he will be taking an unnecessary chance. Before we go any further, Wright, here is your weapon and holster. I suggest you strap it on now before we get to the area."

Gustoff grabbed the weapon and said, "I am in charge; I wear the gun, not him, he is only interested in other people's women."

The first sergeant had a smile on his face and muttered, "It's been fun, while it lasted."

Buck parked the bus, and we were off with Gustoff leading the way with me and the old man in the back.

I whispered, "Do not leave the area; this will not take long."

While Gustoff went under the wire, I looked through the infrared goggles to find out where the ambushes were set up and handed the goggles back to Summerall. The bogies were spread through a tight 10 yard wide swath about 300 yards in front of us. One soldier was a point man about 20 yards in front of the rest of the squad. I whispered to Gustoff that it looks clear.

By the way we were walking we would be at the point man in two or three minutes. As soon as I saw him, I buckled Gustoff's knees with my knees from the rear and placed my gun on his left temple. He pulled his weapon out and shot backwards with his thumb on the trigger, instantly damaging my ear drums and spraying my neck with hot blank fragments.

I fired one shot into his temple, he slumped immediately. He had time to squeeze off another blank before slumping.

The solder on point came out from a tree and shot Gustoff; it took all my strength to hold him up as my shield. I waited until the soldier was less than 10 feet away before dropping him with a shot to the heart. Another soldier ran up firing his rifle, hitting Gustoff several times; and he got the same, one bullet in the heart. Two more soldiers came out from there hiding places firing as fast as they could, squeezing off round after round and this time gutting Gustoff. They must have thought both of us were dead as I waited until they were within three feet of me and two more rounds from my pistol found their targets.

The other soldiers did not want anything to do with this fight. A Russian officer loudly ordered the men to rush me, and as they were too slow to respond he shot two of them as they ran the other way. Two more ran towards me and I emptied the two remaining bullets into their chests. I grabbed Gustoff's pistol and placed mine in his hand. His gun of blanks was resting on top of his head. I figured that if my calculations were right, there were at least two soldiers left, four at the most. The remaining soldiers were too far back and couldn't see what was going on. During this mayhem I took Gustoff's passport out of his back pocket and replaced it with the forged one.

Gustoff was shot so many times he wasn't leaking oil anymore. I called to them in Russian for the remaining soldiers to come help me. The Russian officer in the distance stepped out into a clearing and started walking towards me with two soldiers following behind.

When he was a few feet away he looked at me in Russian clothes and Gustoff in American jeans and was satisfied that the right man was dead. I told him, still in Russian, "Well done; you have killed the enemy agent called Billy Wright. I am Alexander Gustoff and have to go back to continue my duties in the West." He hugged me and called me a true comrade. I didn't look back as I faded into the forest, back towards the border.

When I got back to the bus I said, "Let's get out of here before the Russian Air Calvary gets here and recognizes this bus. I sold the Russian officer a story that he really did believe that Billy Wright is now dead; and to prove it, his corpse and passport are in Russian hands.

Summerall asked, "How many bullets were shot? It sounded like a war out there. How many soldiers were involved? From looking through the infrared goggles it looked like a full squad."

"Well sir, there are six Soviet soldiers dead, not counting Gustoff. The two main goals were completed. We got rid of the mole and planted a falsehood that I am now dead."

"Who killed Gustoff?"

"Gustoff played his part very well acting as my shield. He probably has at least 30 Russian pieces of lead in him."

Summerall said to Buck, "Take us home sergeant. Wright, get those bloody clothes off and put my spare uniform on."

On the way back to the Bad Aibling Base and being exhausted, I must have fallen asleep before we hit the highway. The last thing I remembered was going through the trees on our little bus as someone was talking. Summerall was trying to wake me as we were parked in front of the barracks. After taking a stale cold box lunch up to my room to eat, and wanting to soak in a long hot bath to relax before eating the lunch on my bed, I was ready for a little more sleep when someone knocked on my door.

Isla came into my room and asked where Gustoff was. After telling her he was dead, she broke down and cried. He may have been mean to her, but he was the only familiar face while over here or back in Langley. Consoling her wasn't helping; she went back to her room to be alone.

At breakfast the next morning she sat quietly and the rest of us did the same to show we understand how she felt. Isla wanted to go back to the room where as we had to get another debriefing out of the way. General Neuhofer arrived in the afternoon to be briefed by Summerall and myself. Isla stayed in her room all day without joining us for lunch or supper. The next morning she was missing and Summerall asked if I would go see what is going on.

I said to him, "I have an uneasy feeling that she may feel trapped here without Gustoff. I suggest we let her go home to see friends and relatives. Isla is worth keeping or cultivating, but not at the expense of having her feel she is all alone."

"Okay Wright, we have to figure out how to get her back to Russia without the KGB knowing about it."

"I thought about her well-being all night and how to help her. This is risky but we should call the number Gustoff was calling from the hotel and tell them Isla needs some time with her family. I will deliver her to Prague after visiting her friends in Plzen to fly to Moscow, if the Russians can have her ticket at the Aeroflot counter. I would go back to the West and wait for her to fly into New York in two or three weeks. They would have to have a ticket at Aeroflot's ticket counter in Frankfurt for me the same day she flies back. I believe it will work; and if it doesn't, we have done the best we could do for her."

"Okay Wright, that sounds like a good plan; go sell it to her and see what her response is. I will wait to hear back from you before we take the appropriate next step. You are really taking an unnecessary risk going back so soon."

"Yes sir, it is risky; but if she can be used later in setting up a Moscow base it will be worth it."

# Chapter 15

## One Peccadillo Too Many

Isla was hesitant to let me into her bedroom as she only had a towel on after getting out of the bath. She thought that was wonderful that I would take her to catch a flight home. Isla got up to hug me before I left the room with her heavy bath towel falling to the floor.

She kissed me for a very long time and asked in a school girl fashion, "Billy, please be gentle with me, I am still feeling quite fragile."

Her pale white, well-defined curvy naked body looked very inviting, and was stopping me from thinking about Nicola. I only thought about setting up an operation center in Russia. It was dastardly thinking, but exciting with the chance of having an accomplice who would help in acquiring a way into the Russian Intelligence community. We stayed together long enough to miss breakfast and got dressed in time to join the team for lunch.

At lunch I told the team that Isla wanted to go home for a while and I would take her to Czechoslovakia to see friends; and she would then continue on to

Moscow to be with family. She knows she has to act out that I am Alex, without her friends seeing me and finding out about the plot.

We made the call to the Russian contact and put into motion the action. The team had to buy a motorcycle to replace the other one. This was to be our mode of transportation and with the heavy leather biker's suit on and goggles, no one will be any wiser as to who I am.

Isla wanted to shop for an outfit to wear on the plane. I told her we couldn't take any luggage with us and would shop in Prague the day before she flies out.

The bike was bought on the bus along with team members when we left for Bratislava. We got to the crossing point and were in the forest pushing the bike four hours after leaving the ASA Base. Isla noticed spots of dried blood on the path and wanted to know if this was the place Alex died. It was but I told her no; we had passed it farther back. That seemed to be okay with her and wasn't morbid or sad. At the road the coast was clear as it let us continue to our first stop. I dropped her at the cafe where I was arrested earlier and gave her enough Czech money to hire someone to take her to Prague, where she was to meet me at the Hotel Jalta in two days.

I ended up at the Hotel Botanika. When Lenka heard the motorcycle, she ran out and opened the barn door to hide the bike. We were in the kitchen when her parents drove up with supplies and joined us in having a pot of tea. We helped get the shopping in after the obligatory kisses and handshakes. As soon as the supplies were in, Lenka and I took Sasha into the forest to have a walk before dinner. Later that night, Lenka said that the students often stop in for a drink on the way to their headquarters.

Two days later I left for the Gypsy village to see Topol and exchange dollars into rubles. He was very glad to see me and told me his daughter has found a nice Gypsy boy to go out with.

I told him, "I am glad, too."

He laughed out loud and said, "English, you were almost family. I like that she has found one of her own, though you would have been a good Gypsy, no."

With plenty of rubles in my pocket, I went to meet up with Isla and see Andrea. In the Jalta I told

Andrea about a girl who was meeting me here. She was curious if it was my girlfriend from London.

Isla got to the hotel late and saw me and Andrea in the bar having a good time. This seemed to annoy Isla, and she wanted to go to her room, not our room. Andrea, being a good concierge, showed her to the room next to mine.

I should have kept the relationship with Isla professional and took the chance of her not wanting to continue the CIA training.

The next day we shopped for a Samsonite suitcase so her new clothes and toiletries were in something that would keep them safe. She never tired of trying on different outfits and having to have my approval. She wanted to dress like some of the London Mods she seen in magazines.

We went downstairs to have a drink before dinner when she said, "Billy, I am sorry for acting stupid last night. Seeing my boyfriend with a beautiful woman was more than I could handle."

Oh brother, this isn't going as planned, and I don't see how to get out of this feeling of being trapped. There was too much work to do to start a clandestine relationship with a fellow agent. That night she turned frosty again when I told her I felt a cold coming on.

When we said goodbye at the airport, I said, "Remember Isla, Gustoff is alive and you will meet him in New York in three weeks. If you decide to stay longer, call me at this number to let whoever answers the phone know. I will not be able to call you back with the fear of being found out. Goodbye and have a wonderful time in Russia."

I left for the border and ran into a roadblock on the outskirts of Cheb. It was time to see if my Russian was good enough to convince the soldiers I was Alex Gustoff. The Russian officer in charge read my papers and let me go. An hour and a half later I was at the path and pushing the bike through the forest.

Back inside the ASA office the old man wondered why I didn't ask for money on my last assignment. I informed him that there was money leftover from the last mission.

After the morning debriefing, I left the motorbike at the base and drove my car to the Frankfurt headquarters and another meeting with General Neuhofer. That evening I arrived back in the London flat, and was met by Nicola as she was phoned by

General Simpson's staff as to when I was arriving. She had a steak and kidney pie cooked with mashed potatoes and thick brown gravy. It was the best food I had eaten in a long time. After we ate, we went to the local pub to relax in a friendly happy atmosphere with lots of Cockneys chattering away.

Back in the flat we snuggled up in the warm bed out of the cold air in the room. We made plans for Christmas, if I were back from an assignment that was yet to be formulated.

Between working with the Cambridge team and General Simpson, along with spending time with Nicola, the three weeks before meeting Isla in New York made the time go quickly.

# Chapter 16

## Russia, the Next Affair

Nicola and her parents gave me a lift to catch my flight to New York to rendezvous with Isla coming in from Moscow a couple of hours after my plane landed. The flight with favorable winds was early. I went to the observation deck to watch for Isla just as the Russian jet pulled up to the ramp parking area. When I spotted her, she was at the top of the steps with her Mod outfit on looking quite stylish. She looked over to the people on the deck and waved as she saw me waving.

When Isla came through immigration and out into the arrivals hall she was bursting with energy, happy to be back in the States I assumed. We embraced as if we haven't seen each other for years. A CIA black sedan picked us to go to Washington DC to their headquarters, and to meet with General Thibodeau.

When we met Thibodeau he let Isla and I know what was expected of us for the next 30 days. He had her taken to the farm and I would not see her again until she had completed the course.

Thibodeau went over a scenario involving Isla, myself and the ambassador's wife as operatives in

Russia, based out of Moscow. He wasn't ready to divulge the assignment today, but would be ready to discuss it the day before Isla was released from Langley.

The firm had me booked on the Delta/Pan Am flight from Dulles to London that evening with a return ticket in four weeks. I was ordered to resume the second phase of my being tutored in the London flat with writing the Russian language.

Within two days of getting to the flat, Brumhilda showed up to start the course. After being let in, she brushed me aside and bolted up the stairs calling out in Russian, "Come on, get a move on, we only have a few weeks to get you writing like a Russian." I was not going to enjoy this and rather be shot at through trees in the Czech Republic than be bossed around by this bully.

The only respite I had was the weekends were free to be with Nicola as the weekends flew by, and the five-day week dragged by. A double dash of Scotch and soda at lunch was needed to get through the afternoon sessions.

After the four weeks I could write "see Jack run" in Russian, but somehow that wasn't going to get me into the Kremlin. After saying goodbye to Nicola and London, I was in CIA headquarters, jet lagged and curious what this new assignment was.

Thibodeau and I went to lunch at his golf club in Virginia, and at the bar he ordered a double Scotch with soda on the side. I ordered the same with him looking surprised.

I said, "That cocktail got me through the roughest month of my life."

I asked him, "Just what do you have in store for me or more bluntly do you have my next assignment orders?"

"No, we are not ready to brief you. General Neuhofer is doing the donkey work on this one, which will require the ASA network help to get your Ops center off and running in Moscow. We will know in a month or six weeks at the most."

"I would like to have Christmas off, if possible, and could be ready to go by the time the Russian New Year's celebrations starts."

"I will communicate your wishes to the ones involved; let's eat, you have to have the dish of the season. It is pheasant under glass."

The general was trying to tell me that the next assignment was still being worked on and that all I needed to know for now was to get ready to be Colonel Rasstoff. Cuba was also a possibility for a covert assignment as a Russian colonel.

We met Isla the next afternoon when she walked off the farm. She was so engrossed with a tall, blond hair recruit, she didn't notice us. Thibodeau commented that she looked happy with that fella. We were introduced to him and hoped that he could speak Russian or any Russian dialect.

Her new friend joined us for dinner at the Hilton; we got to know him and liked him very much. His parents were Jewish and were from Ukraine. He spoke Russian fluently. This may be the find that Thibodeau was looking for to help with the Russian connection.

Isla introduced her friend, "Billy I would like for you to meet Petro Apostolic or as he is called in America, Peter Post. Peter was the best at everything, all types of languages. Billy, he knows about you and me. I am so sorry Billy; I like him more now and will not hurt you for anything."

"I am so happy for you two and would like to invite you to London anytime you want to visit."

General Thibodeau said, "Let's go to the bar Wright, and get some Champaign to celebrate these two graduating off the farm."

At the bar he said, "You dodged another bullet that could have cost you your life or relationship with Nicola, which I and mother like very much. When are you going to get married and settle down?"

"When you stop giving me assignments, General. You know, I never so 'no' to you."

"Blame it on me; you don't want to get married. I bet you are scared to settle down or are you just plain yellow. Did you mention to your fiancé that a trip to Russia was being worked on? No you didn't, I was right, you are afraid of her."

He roared with laughter all the way back to the table.

We celebrated and studied Peter all night. I was jealous with his good looks, his height and most of all, his demeanor; so suave without knowing it. I was positive, I hated him. The general and I agreed he has to be ours and pulled in before the boys from the South America team recruits him.

Printed in the United States
By Bookmasters